ALU

The Guardia.

Trev Dube

DEDICATION

For all those who dare to connect the dots looking forward

ACKNOWLEDGMENTS

Thank you to my friends and family for walking this journey with me, and for all your amazing support and encouragement.

Chapter 0

Origins: Legacy of the Cryoscriptorium

In the midst of legends, two courageous souls Asanda and Camille scrawled in the margins of old books in the hallowed corridors of the Cryoscriptorium. Hidden chambers and long-lost volumes held the answers to the mysteries that captivated Asanda, a dedicated futurist, and Camille, a bright physicist. Their love and burning curiosity drove them to seek them out.

A story about powerful sea creatures called the Guardians held their attention. It was believed that these beings, on their way to cosmic enlightenment, travelled the legendary Orca Roads, routes known only to the enlightened. The warnings that Asanda and Camille were not the Chosen Ones for such dangerous missions went unheeded as they became fixated in solving the riddles surrounding these Roads.

They were elated when Asanda found out she was pregnant, thanks to the successful ART procedure. Their decision to establish a family was based on a deeply held desire to experience the joy of welcoming new life into their lives. Asanda looked at Camille with tear-filled eyes, she knew that this child would be raised in the embrace of love and care, surrounded by the wisdom of their cherished Cryoscriptorium. Sitting in the peaceful corners of the library, they read aloud stories of amazing adventure, dreaming of the day they could share their Quest with their little one.

The old athenaeum, which would later become Aluta's sanctuary, echoed with the sound of his first cries. His mothers, captivated, would spin him on an endless adventure between the lofty bookcases adorned with windows leading to fantastical realms. While they perused each aisle as a family, they stoked his insatiable appetite for information.

Gleaming with unbridled wisdom, Asanda's eyes reflected the exhilaration of discovery. In the meantime, Camille considered the enormous consequences of having such esoteric ability, her thoughts swirling like a whirlwind. Their quest went beyond simple understanding; it connected them to the past, shone a light on the way to the future, and wove fate into the intricate fabric of history. Tragically, that changed. The legendary Roads beckoned to Asanda and Camille with whispers of old power. As they set out on their last quest to discover the secrets of the Roads, they left Aluta in the care of Buntu, his beloved.

Only those possessing the spirit of a Guardian could make it through the Roads that took Aluta's parents, according to the stories. However, the solitary youth would not submit to a destiny that demanded giving up on any possibility of reuniting. The stories Buntu told him about Orca Guardians who travelled the stars, sharing knowledge between realms, were like a lifeline to him.

As he settled into his new home amidst the seemingly infinite aisles and archives of the Cryoscriptorium, Aluta took comfort in the knowledge that he would never be alone there. Whispered tales of Guardians traversing the Roads between realms lingered in his heart. Like they had called out to his parents before their tragic journey, they would eventually summon him when the time was right. As he answered their call, all he could have wished was that it would not be his last.

Planet Bantuve, home of Aluta, was a frozen wasteland teeming with life, perched on the edge of the galaxy and embraced by the starry embrace of the dark, empty space. Here, in the perpetual dusk, Aluta stands with his silhouette against the spectral aurora borealis. He has stunning brown skin that soaks up the weak light from a faraway sun, and dreadlocks that are as colourful as a star's corona tumble over his shoulders. With a subtle intensity, his gaze surveys the horizon, his pupils sparkling with nebula iridescence. He exemplifies the ferocity of his planet and stands as a symbol of determination in the face of impending doom.

The myths and stories talked about how the Chosen Guardian will travel the Orca Roads to bring knowledge from other realms and the stars back to Bantuve. Aluta started to see that answers to Bantuve's climatic catastrophe might lie in discoveries made in distant galaxies as he read the scientific notes his moms had left behind.

Who knows? Maybe some extra-terrestrial race has figured out how to harness fusion power or found crops that can grow on the carbon dioxide that Bantuve's atmosphere has trapped over the years. Despite the difficulty of the decisions that were necessary to restore their world, the solutions lay in the depths of space. Aluta was determined to fulfil his parents' dreams of becoming an expert on the Orca Roads so that he could return with the wisdom to save Bantuve from its current predicament and bring back its former glory and hope for a better future.

In the hushed tales passed down through generations, Aluta embodied the destiny of a selected sailor who would face the unforgiving depths and rise as the messenger of a new age. These stories, which are an integral part of Bantuvian mythology, offered a glimmer of optimism among the darkness of their reality.

The Orca Roads were both a source of excitement and dread for Bantuve, a planet on the verge of catastrophic transformation. The unforgiving sea had taken a heavy toll on its inhabitants. Still, the depths of this mystery may hold clues to redemption that only the "one" can decipher.

Climate change was a dark cloud over Bantuve, and it was getting progressively more oppressive by the day. A monument to the planet's failing core, the glaciers that had stood as silent guardians for aeons now sobbed rivers of grief. In the face of mounting floods, the once-great Cryoscriptorium, a repository of invaluable historical records and artefacts, was in danger of disappearing forever.

The myth of the "one" took on added significance during these turbulent times. Aluta, who grew up in the protective arms of the

Cryoscriptorium, came to represent this optimism. Along the Orca Roads, he was on a mission—not merely to learn more about the world or find his fate, but to find a method to save his people's homeland from the catastrophic effects of climate change.

Amidst the heaviness of doubt and the flicker of hope, the inhabitants of Bantuve observed. In addition to being their protector, Aluta personified their strength, bravery, and will to overcome the challenges presented by the elements and the passage of time.

The ocean stretched out before Aluta, a blank slate filled with unknowns and perils, yet the murmurs of Bantuve conveyed a message of faith. I had trust in the 'one' who would venture into the depths, I had faith in the knowledge that would be gained, and I had faith in the future where their world could be healed, its beauty and harmony restored.

With the aspirations and anxieties of a people longing for deliverance, Aluta, the selected son of Bantuve, ventured off to follow the Orca Roads, a route marked by myth and optimism.

The legends of Buntu, the Librarian who took care of Aluta after his parents died, reverberate in his memory as he stares out at the frozen wasteland. These tales describe Orca Roads that snake through the depths and lead to uncharted regions. Aluta is about to leave this world, and at this hour he will go beyond the familiar and into the infinite mysteries that lie beyond. As a symbol of Earth's long history of interstellar communication, the legendary orca Zara breaks the surface with a spray of water filled with stardust. Long have her melodies, crafted from the tapestry of oceanic recollections, led Aluta to this brink of fate.

From my vantage point far above the cosmic drama of light and dark, Enchanté je m'appelle Extraterrestre, tu peux m'appeler X. Now back to our Guardian's odyssey in which I play the role of both subject and narrator my spirit is not of the sea or the ice, but of the space between the stars. Before we get back to the story let me introduce you to Qaqamba, or just Q, she's an ever-shifting constellation of possibilities as she flits in and out of quantum realities. Q sees Aluta as a quantum symphony, where each note represents a step towards unfathomable futures. "He is the light in the darkness," she murmurs, her voice in perfect harmony with the universe. "Ah, Q, you are ever-changing, so tied to the ebb and flow of possibility, but I stand here, the ever-present observer. While she spins quantum tales in quantum scales I construct cosmic narratives in cosmic scales."

An awakening of Aluta, the possible keeper of Bantuve's legacy, and of the endless paths that lie ahead—not with a step, but with a leap into the embrace of the universe—marks the beginning of the journey. Aluta's saga begins at the intersection of eternity and the fleeting moment of now, guided by the wisdom of Buntu and accompanied by the song of Zara.

From the shores of Bantuve, a tale is about to unfold—a chronicle that extends into the great unknown, an odyssey of a guardian whose fate is written in the stars, as the auroras bow to the emerging dawn and the ice shimmers with the promise of the journey. Aluta, his breath tinged with adventure, steps towards the ocean's call.

The icy winds carried the chants of his people, a melodic tapestry of hope and farewell. As Aluta stood at the precipice of the known, the Glacial Maw stretched out before him like a gaping portal to other worlds. He turned to Buntu, the lines on the elder's face deep like the ancient crevasses surrounding them.

"Buntu," Aluta's voice remained steady, a reflection of his determination, but a faint wave of unease suggested the storm brewing inside. His eyes, a dazzling array of colours, revealed the burden of his unspoken fear: the terrifying prospect of his destiny replicating that of his parents, who had been consumed by the same adventure he was about to undertake. "Will the melodies of our people lead me through the vast expanse of space, or will their echoes disappear into the depths, just like my parents did?"

With a strong grip on the young guardian's shoulder, Buntu, whose words had been a guiding light for Aluta's troubled mind, placed his ancient and limitless gaze on Aluta. "Aluta, our songs are more than just melodies; they are the whispers of the ancestors, the resonating pulse of Bantuve itself," Buntu said. "They continue beyond the horizon of our planet and into space, where they chime in harmony with the cosmos' rhythm. The dreams, resilience, and perseverance of our people are within you. Even in the deepest stillness, the music coursing through your veins will lead the way."

Inhaling deeply, Aluta's chest rose as if he were trying to hold Buntu's words in his heart. A spark of determination lit up in his eyes, a silent promise to return from the Orca Roads with the bravery and love of his mothers, to bring the wisdom they had been searching for but could not find. Amid his fears, he felt a newfound faith—faith in the songs of his people, in Zara's guiding hand, and in the path that ultimately belonged to him.

As he bowed low before the Maw, Aluta cast one last look around the assembly. The cries of his people trailed behind him, a vivid reminder of the life he was leaving behind, the life that would later become the bedrock of his journey.

Immersed in the frigid waters, he could make out the haunting chants that had bound him to Bantuve. Down below, where light could not penetrate, the melodies of his people's songs blended with Zara's heavenly voice, leading him further into the universe.

Aluta was embraced by Zara in the dark waters where legends became reality. Zara's towering stature stood out against the abyss they were about to cross, and the chill that crept into his bones served as a constant reminder of how vast the emptiness was. However, the warmth of their bond, which was rooted in Bantuve itself, kept the chill at bay.

"Zara," Aluta said, his voice barely audible above the water as it travelled across the finite network of their mutual comprehension. "I...I am terrified. Rather than fearing the unknown, I am afraid of changing into someone I am not."

"Aluta, in the dance of the cosmos, nothing is lost, only transformed," the orca sang, her notes weaving a tapestry of solace and bravery that echoed through the depths. "No matter how many universes we merge into, the essence of you, the soul that resides in the water with me right now, will never change."

Aluta could feel Zara's song pulsating in time with his heartbeat as they made their way through the tunnels that held the Orca Roads; each pulse seemed to propel him closer to his destiny, a note in the symphony of time that they were about to become a part of.

"Uhm ...no matter how far apart we are, will you still be at my side?" He inquired, his anxiety palpable in the background of his mind.

"Always," Zara reassured, her voice carrying the weight of countless years of experience. "Our connection goes beyond just being physically near. If eternity exists I will always be by your side."

Aluta saw that they were not just travelling through space, but through the fabric of existence when they drew near the core of the Orca Roads, when the waters started to shimmer with the light of other suns and worlds. The gap was filled with the melodies of a thousand oceans.

"I am prepared," Aluta announced, speaking more to himself than Zara. "For Bantuve, for the wisdom that persists beyond, I am prepared."

As a result of that confirmation, the Orca Roads swung wide before them, revealing a myriad of possibilities in the whirling currents. Aluta felt his final traces of uncertainty dissolve, giving way to a determination as expansive as the voyage that lay ahead.

As they continued on their journey, he and Zara silently promised the universe that they would seek knowledge, understand it, and then return with the wisdom of the cosmos. Aluta, encouraged by his people's legends and traditions, now faced the ocean's raw power, which had both nurtured and tested his ancestors. The weight of the sea enveloped him as he dove into the abyss, a sobering reminder that this realm was not for the unchangeable.

The intensity of the pressure increased, as if trying to punish him for his incursion. Aluta gasped for breath, his body straining against the depths that threatened to engulf him in a deadly embrace. Panic, an unseen killer, started to obscure his vision, casting a shadow over the chants of his people, which now appeared like faraway fantasies.

"Hold on, Aluta," Zara's voice echoed within him, resonant and unyielding. "Trust in the transformation; it is your birth right, your destiny." Zara's strong presence moved near, offering refuge from the approaching darkness.

In the face of mounting uncertainty, Aluta's efforts were increasingly difficult and his journey through the Orca Roads increasingly perilous; the dark depths of the ocean's core were a devouring emptiness, where hope appeared too flimsy to sustain, and where the strongest resolve could waver.

In the space between belief and dread, his mothers' faces emerged from the water, not as ghosts but as genuine beings. They did not utter a word; words were not necessary. Their eyes, illuminated by a mystical light, communicated a message of oneness and love without speaking a word.

"We are here, Aluta," they appeared to say, their shapes glowing and peaceful in the depths of the abyss. "Our voyage along the Orca Roads continues within you. The song that leads you and the courage that keeps you going are in our hands."

Their ethereal embrace brought Aluta comfort, and his determination hardened. The Orca Roads, he understood, were more than just passages across the underworld; they were portals into the past and future, linking him to the stories of others who had gone before.

At that terrifying moment, when Aluta's determination faltered, something moved in the water. Q's energy came together, her quantum lights a wonder in the depths. "You are not alone," she said. "The ocean tests you, but it will also yield to you." Ah, Aluta, you are the true one."

Aluta felt time itself in the Orca Roads, a whirlwind of possibilities where the past, present, and future danced eternally with one another. As he pushed through the crack, his body changed drastically, shrinking and adapting, taking in the knowledge of the depths.

Aluta's human physiology became one with the orca's, the master of the sea, as Zara's melodic thrumming guided him. His organs shifted, his lungs condensed, and his senses heightened, attuned to the vibrations and subtle shifts of the underwater currents, reflecting the orca's own evolutionary mastery of the deep.

"The human form is so delicate, yet so remarkably versatile," X pondered, their thoughts lost in the vast expanse of the night sky. "To see it now, compressing, adapting—such marvellous resilience." Like the stars and planets, themselves, it is always shifting and changing but ultimately lasting.

With the strength of his aquatic shape at his back, Aluta swam through the aeons of time with the elegance befitting an aquatic being. His eyes, which had previously only seen the surface, could now take in the whole fabric of existence, with each thread acting as a pulse, a beating heart of the cosmos.

"Observe how every decision and deed echoes through the ages," Q said, her voice resonating with the subatomic. "On your voyage, every hop along the Orca Roads is a stroke on the masterpiece that is life."

He was more than just a wanderer; he was a channel for the knowledge of centuries past, a carrier of the tales that would mould the future; and his mind, previously filled with thoughts of leaving and loss, suddenly opened to the magnificence of his mission.

Aluta witnessed the birth of stars, the fall of civilizations, and the silent poetry of galaxies colliding in a dance as old as the universe itself as the transition reached its zenith and the Orca Roads unfolded before him in a display that defied description. Time, which was no longer a linear path, revealed itself in layers and dimensions that Aluta had never imagined.

Within the sacred space of the Orca Roads, he experienced a magnificent metamorphosis. His body, a marvel of human ingenuity, started a breath-taking metamorphosis, not a shrinkage but an evolution, which enabled him to flourish in the deepest recesses of the ocean. It was a natural wonder, but there was more to it than that—a hint of the celestial hand that had led his people in the stories of Buntu.

Zara, an orca whose long lineage had conquered the depths of the ocean, weaved her voice into Aluta's genetic code, singing a song of transformation. Aluta's body adapted, his internal organs becoming as hardy as those of the deep sea, and his lungs absorbing the orcas' wisdom about how to use oxygen so efficiently and how to endure pressures that would break the weak.

"The human vessel, amazing in its flexibility, now harmonises with the depths," X remarked, a hint of awe in their celestial delivery. "It is not compression that defines this moment but an expansion—a broadening of capability, a deepening of connection to the lifeblood of the ocean." replied Q. "In the depths, Aluta becomes more than a sum of biological processes. He embodies the fluidity of existence itself, each cell a reflection of the universe's boundless adaptability," she said, her observations being a link between the visible and invisible.

The Orca Roads spread out before Aluta like light ribbons as he delved deeper under Zara's instruction; each road led to a different era and location. Aluta was in awe of the feeling as his body became exquisitely tuned to his surroundings. Born of Bantuve's ice yet recreated in the image of the stars, he was no longer limited to the terrestrial, but now he was a celestial being.

"The human form, ever so malleable, aligns now with the pulse of the deep, echoing the eternal resilience of the cosmos," said X. "Within

Aluta stirs the legacy of terrestrial and celestial realms, a symphony of natural history and cosmic destiny playing out in the theatre of his soul."

Aluta gasped his way to the surface of the water, and the inhabitants of Bantuve who had gathered on the coast burst into jubilant celebration. The sea had not consumed their Guardian like others before him; rather, he had emerged from the depths anew, prepared to face his fate.

With a look of pure joy and pleasure on his face, Buntu rose to his feet. "Aluta, my boy, you have become our hope," he proclaimed, his voice resonating with the congregation. "You have answered the ocean's challenge and emerged as our Protector."

As Aluta felt the burden of his new position descend over him, he glanced around at the eager faces. "I am here to serve, to protect not only Bantuve but all the worlds that are waiting for us to come to their aid," he replied with conviction.

"Aluta, you have proven your determination. The ocean has tried you, and you have triumphed," Q remarked, her voice radiating warmth and wisdom.

With a graceful dive, Zara soared above the water, her joy evident in the splash that accompanied her. Her voice blended with the Bantuvians' chants as she sang, "Together, we will journey through the Orca Roads. Together, we will seek the wisdom of the cosmos."

The group broke into a chant, an old tune that talked of wisdom, protection, and journeys. A melodic link between the people and the protector who stood before them, the beat ebbed and flowed with the tides.

At Aluta's side, Buntu brandished the Mark of the Guardian, a glowing paint made from bioluminescent marine organisms. In a ritual as ancient as the stories themselves, he steadily marked Aluta's forehead. The glowing mark, representing Aluta's connection to the celestial bodies, shone against his beautiful brown skin.

Buntu chanted the words of dedication as he painted the emblem. "With this mark, you are forever bound to the heart of Bantuve, to the pulse of the universe. You are Aluta, our Guardian, the bridge between our world and the unknown."

There was a cacophony of splashes, clicks, and melodies as all the marine life got in on the party. Underneath, gentle giants sang their approbation as dolphins danced on the waves and fish leaped in glittering arcs. His dear moms, Asanda and Camille, who were inseparable in spirit and love, would be overjoyed to see their son, Aluta, embraced by the sea's jubilant tribute, a symbol of the diversity of love and family.

Aluta embraced his people and their fate as he stretched his arms towards the heavens. "I am Aluta, Keeper of the Orca Roads, Guardian of Bantuve and the Universe."

The people of Bantuve erupted in jubilation, their voices harmonising in a chorus that echoed through the heavens. Those who had endured the loss of loved ones at the hands of the ocean's embrace now found comfort in Aluta's triumph and purpose. They perceived in him the fulfilment of their tales, the start of a fresh chapter in Bantuve's narrative. As the sun set, the inhabitants of Bantuve continued to sing, their voices weaving a tapestry of optimism and bravery. Meanwhile, Aluta gazed into the infinite expanse of space, secure in the knowledge that he would forever be accompanied by the essence of his home, the resilience of his people, and the assurance of a protector who would resist the ebb and flow of any crisis that endangered the fragile equilibrium of existence.

As the Bantuvian Council and Aluta embarked on a massive strategy to counteract the dangers of climate change the following morning in the midst of the Cryoscriptorium Lab's flurry of activity and innovation, each member—a specialist in their own domain—wound a web of solutions, spinning a yarn of hope and sustainability for the future.

Engineers worked tirelessly on advanced solar panels and wind turbines, capturing the relentless energy of Bantuve's environment. In a corner of the lab, physicists delved into the secrets of nuclear fusion, seeking to emulate the stars' power. Technologists tinkered with prototypes for transmitting energy wirelessly, dreaming of a future unshackled from the confines of cables. Designs for zero-emission vehicles dotted the workspace, alongside models of efficient public transit systems.

A team dedicated to audacious ideas sketched plans for space elevators, envisioning a world connected to the cosmos. Scientists experimented with enhanced carbon capture technologies, envisioning a future where the air was free of excess carbon. Biologists and engineers collaborated on artificial trees, capable of outperforming nature in absorbing CO_2. Agronomists and geneticists pooled their knowledge to revolutionize agriculture with lab-grown meat and resilient crops.

Economists and policy experts developed and argued for economic frameworks that prioritise wellness for the planet and people. Environmentalists outlined models such as the doughnut economy, emphasizing regeneration and equality. Educators drafted new curricula, infusing future generations with knowledge and respect for their planet. Sociologists strategized on fostering a cultural shift towards sustainable living and minimal waste. Diplomats planned to forge international alliances, setting targets for reducing greenhouse gas emissions. Tech specialists designed global monitoring systems, ensuring accountability in environmental practices. Scientist researched geoengineering, aware of its potential as a last resort against climate change.

Each project at the Cryoscriptorium Lab was a leap forward in the fight to save their planet, and in the middle of it all stood Aluta, the guardian, whose voyage through the Orca Roads had kindled a fire that now burned fiercely in the hearts of the Bantuvian people.

Chapter 1
Planet on the Brink

Even if the world's busy inhabitants did not hear or see Aluta's initial steps into Civilization One, the planet nonetheless sensed the existence of this new factor in fate's equation. He was astounded and impressed by the civilization that was flourishing before his eyes as it meticulously used the planet's resources. A verdant mosaic interwoven with the city's glass and steel. With their humongous blades slicing through the air, towering wind turbines resembled contemporary monoliths and communicated the transformation of energy. A monument to the civilization's dedication to capturing the sun's limitless energy, solar panels spread out across rooftops and hillsides.

But there was also a sense of pressing need, a tangible strain that hinted at a system that was about to burst. The tension between consumption and conservation was palpable to Aluta, and he pondered the question of how much longer this delicate equilibrium might endure until disaster struck.

"Voilà, he stands at the precipice of innovation and devastation. Such a precarious dance, n'est-ce pas?" X mused, intrigued by the delicate tightrope of technological advancement and ecological awareness the planet maintained. "The equilibrium is dynamic, a continuous play of forces," Q noted. "Aluta's presence is a catalyst, a variable that could tip the scales towards harmony or collapse."

Aluta, who carried Bantuve's wisdom within him, was compelled to explore more and comprehend the complex equilibrium that this world faced. Stepping forward into the centre of the civilization, he inhaled deeply, savouring the air that was brimming with creativity and oxygen.

A civilization that was both firmly grounded in the earth and ambitiously looked to the stars characterised this futuristic globe. Here, among these people, Aluta saw the dangers of excess and the lessons of growth. He could discover the next part of his trip here, and maybe even contribute a chapter as well.

As Aluta meandered across the city, his awe at the technological wonders around him gradually faded, replaced instead by clear signs of imbalance. The air was thick with the aroma of development, but there was also a faint smell of decay, as if the environment were struggling to support its own rapid expansion.

Aluta met Ayodele, a caretaker of the city's Central Arboretum's natural resources. While keeping an eye on data forecasts, she could not make out the bleaker predictions due to the constant blaring of emergency alarms. At the same time as, seismic activity was getting worse, electricity needs kept going up, almost overwhelming the grid. Ayodele watched as her worst fears materialised on the screens.

"What troubles you, steward?" Aluta asked, his voice soft and appealing. The intensity of Ayodele's worry was palpable as she raised her gaze to the sky. "Our world is precariously balanced, guest," she said. "We have come to the brink of technologically harvesting the wind and sun. The Earth may soon be unable to support human consumption."

In agreement, Aluta nodded. "Your advancements are remarkable, but they must not become chains that bind you to a dying world." To which Ayodele replied, "Exactly," her voice betraying her annoyance. "Our civilization has developed a focus on the future, but here we are, on the brink of disaster. The equilibrium we have achieved is precarious."

She had forewarned the council years ago that the city teetered precariously on the brink of disaster. Avalanches begin slowly before they accelerate uncontrollably. The electricity system was also beginning to feel the strain of society's demands placed on it by the biosphere's limited capacity to provide those demands. The first stones of the impending disaster were now falling down the hill.

The abrupt ground tremor that ran through the area cut off their discourse. Alarms went off, creating a clamour that mirrored Ayodele's anxieties. The city's ecological supports were about to be overwhelmed by the soaring energy demands, according to the gloomy projections shown on the screens.

Ayodele gasped, "This is what I feared," but the commotion nearly muted her. "While our systems are strong, they are not impenetrable. We risk disastrous system failures if we do nothing." Asking, "Show me," Aluta persisted. "Perhaps the wisdom of Bantuve can offer a path forward."

The two of them made a beeline for the city's energy nexus, the centre from which all power emanated. As they watched, the mask of order surrounding them started to fall, exposing the harsh truth of a civilisation at war with nature—and failing. With the warning alarms blaring, Ayodele guided Aluta to a quiet grove in the Arboretum, far from the hustle and bustle of the city. This is where she started telling the story of how their world went from being a society that had to deal with nature's unpredictable patterns to one that was about to tap into all of its resources.

"The planet's moods—the droughts, the storms, the quakes—were our undoing long ago," Ayodele started, her voice unwavering in the midst of the mayhem. "Our forefathers found solace in the heavens as they fought the unpredictable weather. In their ideal world they could control the elements according to their desires."

Aluta paid close attention as Ayodele recounted the struggles and victories of the early settlers, the future's potential for unfettered energy flow like rivers, and the danger of losing sight of where their wealth came from.

"Need and ambition propelled us forward," Ayodele went on to say. "We excavated deep into the earth and erected towers to survey the sky for meteorites. We thought we had become on par with the sun when we grasped its essence and stretched out to touch it."

"However, as we progressed," she paused, her expression growing more serious, "we ran the danger of becoming distracted from our role in the universe. What was once our saviour our technology is now a sword that threatens destruction at the first sign of trouble."

A culture that teetered precariously between embracing the blessings of advancement and clinging to its humble beginnings, their climb to power was a complex web of invention and hubris.

"The balance is delicate," Ayodele said, leaving Aluta with a mixture of optimism and despair in his eyes. "We need the wisdom of those who have walked this path before us, who have understood that to wield the power of the elements is not to dominate them, but to coexist with them."

The significance of Ayodele's remarks hit Aluta hard. Her life's work echoed Bantuve's teachings, which emphasised the need of preserving the environment and the fact that human advancement must not come at the expense of it.

Aluta said, "To advance is human," his words dripping with the knowledge of his own culture. "But to do so with foresight, to honour the gifts of nature that is the mark of a truly advanced civilization."

With a nod, the steward took comfort in Aluta's comprehension. By working together, they would overcome the obstacle in their path and get their technical wonders back in sync with the living world's rhythms.

A chaotic symphony of last-ditch efforts replaced the normally tranquil hum of synced technology at the city's energy nexus. Engineers and technicians rushed to stop the catastrophe, their expressions betraying the crushing reality that their civilization's progress was about to collapse.

In the middle of the chaos, Aluta stood with Ayodele at her side as she described the terrible situation. She quietly stated, "The balance of our energy grid is faltering," despite the noisy environment. "We need a new solution, a synthesis of our knowledge and a wisdom we have yet to embrace."

The old Bantuvian mythology, in which reverence for the natural world was not merely an ideal but a necessity for one's very existence, rushed through Aluta's thoughts. Aluta spoke above the din, saying, "In Bantuve, we learned to listen to the whispers of the earth, to harmonise our actions with the rhythm of the world." "Perhaps what is needed is not more control, but a deeper understanding."

Ayodele sought solace in the arboretum's serene atmosphere as experts frantically worked to prevent catastrophe. While she wandered nervously and thoughtlessly among the trees, Aluta offered her comfort. The city had formerly been at nature's mercy, not powering it. Years of disappointment showed on her face as she looked up at him, yet there were also glimmerings of hope behind her eyes.

Ayodele narrated the story of how courageous pioneers of yesteryear had the audacity to hope that engineering could one day free humanity from the clutches of natural disasters like drought and storms. Subterranean pumps were sucking secret reservoirs dry at a rate greater than their ability to refill, as towers began to scrape the skies. The solar towers were so arrogant that they turned the sun's infinite rays into electricity.

It was a lesson we never learned: balance, Ayodele moaned. We continue to disregard the warnings and attempt to manipulate forces that we do not fully understand. Technology can no longer guarantee a rescue for our planet, and it is on the verge of collapse. Dominating nature leads only to mutually assured disaster; we need people with your knowledge.

As the situation deteriorated, Aluta proposed an audacious solution: combining this culture's technological advancements with Bantuve's ideas to establish a mutually beneficial energy system that could respond instantly to changes in human and environmental demands.

The world needs to establish respect as its cornerstone if it is to create a durable equilibrium, which Aluta understood. The ancient concepts of ecosystems that his people cultivated might still be able to turn the city's strained infrastructure into a dynamic and resilient grid, he told Ayodele. If they work together, they may be able to bring the constructed environment back into balance with the living globe.

When Ayodele understood, his expression changed. "A living grid!" she shouted. "One that breathes with the planet, that anticipates and adjusts, rather than merely reacts."

As a result of people's desperation, the concept quickly spread. In a collaborative effort with the engineers, Aluta conceived of a dynamic grid that would mimic the interdependent nature of Bantuve's ecosystems. Following his advice, the engineers devised a bio-integrated power infrastructure that showed promise.

Upon the new system's activation, the energy fluxes started to level out. Once a static system of consumption and supply, the nexus became alive and moved with the planet's natural cycles. As the impending disaster faded into the distance, the panels' red warnings gave way to the serene, balanced hues of blue and green.

After waiting with bated breath, the crowd burst into jubilation. We avoided disaster by embracing nature rather than trying to control it. Aluta's age-old knowledge, together with the civilization's cutting-edge technology, has given rise to a novel way of coexisting with nature.

Ayodele looked over at Aluta, her eyes filled with gratitude. "You have not only saved our world today but have shown us a path to true advancement—a future where technology serves as a bridge to a deeper connection with our planet."

With joy in his heart, Aluta gave a nod. As a family, you will continue a tradition that values the past while also preparing the way for the future. The real indicator of a great society is this concord of progress.

The city, which had been on the verge of collapse, was now flourishing as a result of the newfound knowledge. Knowing he had left this world a little wiser, much more hopeful, and with his objective accomplished, Aluta was ready to continue his trip.

As the sun dipped below the horizon and night fell, the city fell into a new state of peace. There was now a harmonious coexistence between the rapid pace of technological development with the constant buzz of nature. In the middle of it all, Aluta stood as the master weaver of harmony, his soul carrying the wisdom passed down from the Orca Roads that had touched every culture he had the honour of visiting.

There was silence in the grove when Q materialised. "Your actions have woven a new thread into the destiny of this world," she said. With his eyes reflecting the final rays of the setting sun, Aluta turned to her and whispered. "It is the rhythm of the universe that beats within me now."

Up above them, the universe extended like a never-ending painting for X to depict their story. As they observed the situation below, a mischievous grin spread across his face. They murmured from the heavens, "Ah, la symphonie commence, and notre héros an encore changé la mélodie."

The Orca Roads were like a tapestry of space and time itself, drawing Aluta in. Zara's melody beckoned to him, leading him melodically on his next celestial adventure. "The universe is vast, and your path is laced with infinite possibilities," Q said "This harmony you have fostered here is but a prelude to the wonders you will encounter." Aluta made his departure preparations with a nod to Q and a determined heart. Even if his duty here had come to an end, the Guardian's journey had only just begun.

Chapter 2
The Shadows of the Sphere

The glitter of a stellar nebula announced Aluta's approach, casting its astral light across the civilisation that had achieved close connection with its sun. Encased within the gigantic embrace of a Dyson Sphere, the energy of the home star pulsated with the rhythm of a billion lives in this Type II civilization.

The radiant variety that Aluta beheld as he travelled across their realm, which was connected by arteries that channelled captured solar energy, both outstripped and brought together countless worlds and species in its healing light. The light encouraged bioluminescent amphibians to express themselves creatively, while colonies of subterranean fungi used the darkness they absorbed to carve elaborate bioluminescent galleries. There was a cutthroat capitalist marketplace where hundreds of niche enterprises competed for access to limitless clean energy. However, one thing that all of these cultures had in common was their pride in being the first and only networked civilization to harness the power of a star's core to create life as we know it.

An ode to a culture that had grown beyond its cave and seen God face to face, the magnificence of human creativity was on full display. From his vantage point on the viewing deck, Aluta could see the Dyson Sphere's curvature stretching out below him like an infinite horizon. It was an unbelievable sight, a symbol of the limitless possibilities of human advancement.

Built from countless materials sourced from worlds across several systems, the enormous Dyson Sphere that encased their sun was an unparalleled achievement. The ancient builders of the megastructure had assembled its millions of individual panels from crashed planets and asteroids. Encasing the sun would have necessitated enough material to construct a solar array twice the diameter of Pluto's orbit, demonstrating the immense size of this engineering marvel. A lack of backup plans in the event of a Sphere breakdown and the possibility of single-point failures persisted despite the exponential energy gains. Biodomes that could sustain themselves, distributed solar satellites, and a variety of renewable energy sources were among the solutions put out by some.

An audacious vision borne of centuries of hard work astounded Aluta. However, he could not help but notice the underlying ethical unease in the society. Their obsession with achieving unfathomable power was only surpassed by the moral uncertainty surrounding the consequences of their newfound authority.

A voice resonating across the quantum fabric of space and time said, "C'est une prouesse impressionnante," as X deliberated. An entity with heavenly origins like them could not help but admire the creators of such a feat of engineering. Q hinted, "Every photon captured is a story," as her point of view revealed the complex network of energy flows that kept the civilization alive.

"Le progrès n'est pas sans conséquence," X remarked, their tone tinged with a stroke of philosophical humour. "Each choice casts ripples across the canvas of existence, mon ami."

With the trapped star reflected in his eyes, Aluta fixed his gaze on the road ahead. It was a voyage through space and time, but also through the intricate web of moral dilemmas that this alien planet posed.

Stepping forward into the centre of the Sphere, Aluta, the bearer of dynamic balance and knowledge, was prepared to face the moral dilemmas faced by a society that had achieved absolute control over energy. In the pursuit of knowing the real price of advancement, the light was not merely physical, but also mental and spiritual.

There was a cacophony of voices that Aluta could not decipher deep within the culture that had encircled their star. A heated ethical discussion had broken out inside the Dyson Sphere, that magnificent monument of human ingenuity. The once-unified society was now fractured as its members struggled to understand the consequences of their own creation.

A marvel of nearly endless power, the Sphere had lifted billions out of poverty, put an end to scarcity, and given people hope for a better future. Nevertheless, it was also a constraint, as it bound the civilization to just one star, an isolated aberration in the wide universe.

Aluta paid close attention as the people's voices rang out in a mix of optimism and dread.

"Have we become Icarus?" inquired an elderly woman, her reflective eyes reflecting the artificial light. "Flying too close to the sun, only to have our wings of hubris melted?"

"C'est une ironie exquise," said X. "They reach for the stars, only to find themselves bound to one." "Q" interjected "The Sphere's potential is boundless but so too is its capacity to consume."

The burden of the civilization's plight weighed heavily on Aluta's heart. Even though it had propelled them to the peak of Type II civilization status, the Sphere was on the verge of bringing them crashing down. The stars, which they could no longer reach, bore the moral cost of their rise to power.

"Their light is both a beacon and a prison," said X. "To harness a star is to hold fire in your hands—eternally brilliant, eternally burning."

With the society's hopes and dreams on one side and the Sphere's darkness on the other, Aluta found himself in the middle of a cosmic conundrum. It was a philosophical and not just technical test of one's ability to control divine power and the weight of responsibility that accompanies it.

The renowned philosopher Chidike, whose insights were as valuable as the energy that drove their society, was Aluta's final destination on his quest. From his vantage point on the Dyson Sphere, which reflected their society's aspirations and extended out into the night sky, he could see a canopy of unsolved mysteries. Growing up in the artificially endless daylight without ever seeing the real night sky is something that Chidike, an outspoken dissenter, strongly disagreed with. Part of the reason he became so famous was because he had a remarkable knack for expressing the unspoken tension among his people about the possibility of complete collapse under such absolute control.

Aluta began to see the significance of Chidike and his efforts to reestablish their lost heavenly link as he delved into Chidike's accounts of the generations of sacrifices made to elevate the Dyson Sphere. The artists, poets, and environmentalists who opposed the Sphere's monoculture were the cornerstone of his campaign. Because subsequent generations may never lay eyes on the planets that actually contain their ancestry, core believers feared they would lose connection with their roots. Nor could they conceive of kids seeing the night for what it really is: a beautiful phenomenon best experienced directly, not only read about in books. A people who had crossed space and time were now bound to a singular goal by the very accomplishment that had given them hope for the future.

The Sphere's ravenous appetite for minerals, credits, and possibilities, however, allowed businessmen to amass tremendous riches. Rather of seizing the star-spanning opportunities before them, its lobby sought to portray the "celestial conservationists" as naively clinging to the little worlds and limited potentials from whence they sprang. What good would it do for a people to stop discovering the universe so they can reconnect with a small, isolated group that longs for the days of staring into space?

Chidike met with Aluta. "Progress is the pursuit of the horizon," Chidike started, his voice embodying the serene years of contemplation. "Only progress, but how much does it cost? Even though it uses solar energy to power itself, our sphere has obscured the sky it lights up.

With his head a whirlwind of new information and old instructions from Bantuve, Aluta nodded. "The elders speak of balance," he responded. "The eternal waltz between being and not-being. Is the relentless advance of technology causing us to lose our groove?"

With his unwavering fixation on the artificial daylight, Chidike emitted a subtle smile. "For all time, life has been a battle for equilibrium. As we have set our sights on the stars, we have lost sight of the night that gave us the gift of imagination."

A continual reminder of the life it supported and the lives it obscured; the Sphere's hum served as mute evidence to their discussion. The words spoken by Chidike struck a chord with Aluta because they were true and because they mirrored the unease in his own spirit.

"La sagesse est souvent trouvée dans le silence entre les étoiles," said X. "The ethics of progress are not black and white," Q said, her presence subtle but deep. "They are the spectrum of all possible futures, each choice a divergence on the path of destiny."

With a twinkle in his eye, Chidike looked over at Aluta. "The melodies of a celestial realm unbound by star song reside in your hearts, you who have traversed the Orca Roads. Who knows? Maybe it is you who will bring back the wisdom from last night."

Being a link between the long-lost harmony and the future, Aluta felt the burden of his position. "I will carry our dialogue to the stars," he said, "and seek the balance that eludes us."

The Sphere, a tribute to human creativity and a reflection of the questions that would influence their destiny, kept quietly turning as the two figures sat in deep thought.

Aluta and the assembled minds of the civilisation stood in the shadow of the Dyson Sphere, staring up at the gigantic structure that encased their star.

Chidike's remarks had planted the seeds of transformation, and Aluta's arrival had accelerated the development of a fresh comprehension. "We have managed to bring a sun under control," Aluta announced to the gathering. "But we have become its slaves in the process of our conquest. We must now strive for unity with the universe rather than dominance over it."

Because this was such a drastic change from the way they had always done things, the crowd whispered their approval. Aluta advocated a paradigm change, abandoning the Sphere's singularity in favour of a more distributed and environmentally friendly energy strategy.

"Regardez," X thought to themselves. "The child of Bantuve weaves his tale, and deeply listens, as the stars bear witness. The transition will not be without its challenges," Q answered, her presence palpable though unseen. "But the rewards... the potential for a future unbounded by a single star's leash."

Aluta's fervour sparked the imaginations of those in attendance, and his words conjured a future in which their culture was a celestial symphony, with every star and planet contributing a lyric to the cosmic melody.

With a strong and distinct voice, the philosopher Chidike sprang to his feet. "What Aluta says is something that everyone has felt but has been afraid to say. Despite its beauty, our Sphere must not confine us."

Aluta spoke with these idealists who were brimming with plans for future galactic conquests and delivered a sombre warning based on his travels: that civilizations were exalted by pride until it was suddenly deflated. As a result of Aluta's catalysing presence, Chidike's movement gained momentum, and the philosopher witnessed his people halting their relentless growth for the first time in decades. Maybe now, after all they had gone through to eclipse the sky, they would pause long enough to rediscover the wonders that were up there.

They collaborated on an idea for a system of solar harvesters, a constellation of satellites that would harness energy from all the stars in the sky. The ingenious solution acknowledged both their necessities and the reverence for the life-giving suns.

When Aluta saw the people of the society come together, their expressions of joy and determination beaming, his heart was overjoyed. Still, the Sphere would stand as a symbol of their history, marking the turning point from dominance to harmony with the universe.

The stars above appeared to nod as the assembly broke apart, as if the cosmos were on board with the new course of action that humanity had chosen. With Zara by his side, Aluta knew that the Orca Roads were calling him, and that numerous other civilisations were waiting for him to bring his curiosity, wisdom of dynamic balance and collaboration.

As the hum of balanced energy echoed through his bones, Aluta's lengthy shadow stretched across the Dyson Sphere's control dais. A new energy had taken hold, and he could feel it permeating the building all the way to the star at its core. Cooperation brought about a harmony, and both parties understood the need of maintaining a dynamic balance between progress and preservation.

Chidike approached him just as he was about to depart. "Aluta, your words have given us new perspective," she remarked, her voice tinged with optimism. Now we know that the star is more than simply a power plant; it is an integral component of our being, the beating heart of our celestial body.

Aluta nodded, his thoughts consumed by the gravity of their decisions and the power they had to make or break them. "Every culture needs to figure out how to handle this equilibrium," he responded. "To thrive, not just survive."

Next to him, Q raised her voice. "Remember, Aluta, that your actions have consequences, and that there is a quantum dance between cause and effect, as you continue on your path. The choreography is quite subtle."

As X whispered, "Bon voyage, Aluta," "Your path is woven into the fabric of this universe, each thread a story of its own."

Aluta took one last glance at the stars above before making his way to the Sphere's perimeter. Zara, who waited below him, served as a continual reminder of life's ups and downs. The inhabitants of the civilisation gathered to see him leave as he dived into the Orca Roads. He perceived glimpses of their own experiences and perspectives on the cosmos in their eyes. Similar to how Aluta had moulded their future, they had learnt an important lesson that would determine their course of action.

"Until we meet again," Chidike cried out, his philosopher's mind already processing the events of the day and contemplating the next chapter in their shared narrative.

The celestial expanse above mirrored the Bantuve Sea, which eagerly anticipated their descent, as Aluta and Zara embraced each other in the depths with one last leap. They leapt, changing the course of human history and serving as an example for others to follow.

Aluta, a protector of all, continued his long voyage even as the Sphere faded into the distance, bearing the burden of humanity's decisions.

Chapter 3
The Supernova Kiss

As stars are born and die in the cosmic blink of an eye, Aluta's quest finds its next verse in the velvet darkness of space. He finds himself drawn to a culture that has achieved such complete control over the cosmic forces that they have harnessed the untamed energy of their entire galaxy.

Stepping out of the glowing portal a passageway crafted by Zara's age-old aquatic sorcery Aluta stands at the entrance to another dimension. Cities illuminated by the collected light of a million suns reveal a culture that moves to the beat of pulsars before him. The architectural wonders that float in space a beautiful blend of technology and craftsmanship that defies the fundamental law of entropy evidence the grandeur of their accomplishments.

What passes for air in their sky cities is actually the power of contained supernovae, and Aluta is astounded by the sight. The people who live in this galactic kingdom seem to be one with the energy that powers their bodies; their graceful movements mirror the constellations that they revere.

Still, Aluta feels a subtle discomfort despite all this beauty. Despite their mastery over the elements, they are still vulnerable and must keep the delicate balance. It is a culture on the brink of a new era, one that could one day become guardians of the entire cosmos, not just their galaxy.

"Quelle prouesse," X suggests. "They have woven the tapestry of their existence into the very framework of the galaxy," Q notes, her beloved probability trembling at the thought of such a feat.

At this crossroads of authority and duty, Aluta will discover the meaning of star energy mastery and the tools by which to protect a culture that has set its sights on the stars and is now within striking distance. Type III civilizations dwell here, and galactic dominion is but a stepping stone to an even larger journey.

In a cosmos on the brink of anarchy and harmony, the magnificent assembly hall of the Galactic Council stands as a guiding light, directing the energy of innumerable stars into the control of trillions. Aluta sees a display of democracy on a grand scale never before seen. Alien creatures from all throughout the galaxy, with bodies as varied as the planets they were born on, argue passionately about the directions their destiny should take.

Suhail, a being of boundless energy, challenges the council, and Aluta, who is still buzzing from Zara's counsel, listens carefully. "Freedom is the right of every spark of consciousness," Suhail proclaims, his voice resembling a celestial symphony. "Yet, we bind ourselves to the will of the many, sacrificing the desires of the individual for the perceived good of the whole."

The weight of the declaration fills the auditorium, echoing the inaudible voices of many worlds and peoples who are not here. Aluta senses the conflict, a tug between the majesty of this group's power and the eerily familiar nudges of individual ambition.

Thalassa, a matriarch with nebula eyes and an experienced council member, stands up to argue. "Giving up on one's own wants is a prerequisite for star governance. It requires us to think about everyone's welfare. In what other ways may humans safely traverse the vast expanse of space?"

Liraz, an activist whose enthusiasm for self-expression is as brilliant as a supernova, becomes a kindred spirit to Aluta throughout this conversation. With their eyes locking with Aluta's, Liraz argues, "We are not just citizens of stars, but dreamers, artists, lovers." It is a wordless cry for understanding. Defiance shone like a supernova in Liraz, captivating Aluta the minute they first met. Her intense stare revealed a need for comprehension that stirred up long-suppressed feelings of belonging that he had buried under his restless journeys.

He saw the fire in her eyes as she passionately spoke, and he made plans to cross paths with her in the days that followed. Their chemistry blossomed in these serendipitous meetings, where they exchanged hushed looks and argued passionately till dawn.

An X says, "Ah, la liberté," in a serious but humorous voice. "An eternal quandary, as old as the stars themselves." Answering, Q murmurs, "Each choice branches into a new reality," her voice resembling the rustle of cosmic winds. "Yet, how does one choose when the paths are infinite?"

In the midst of this cosmic dispute, Aluta struggles to shake the memories of Bantuve's simpler existence, when the vastness of the ocean represented freedom from the complications of galactic control. Looking for a common thread that might weave together seemingly incompatible ideas, he contemplates Buntu's teachings, the depths of the ocean, and the endless sky.

This is a turning point, a dispute over fundamental questions about philosophy, the nature of reality, and even the nature of government. And while the stars keep an eye on everything, Aluta stands up, prepared to sing with the heavenly choir, and he argues for a dynamic balance between the individual flame and the collective light of the galaxy.

Nia the Rebels' fearless leader observed the delegations of organic life forms with thinly veiled contempt. Unlike the motley palette of flesh and instincts before her, she embodied the pinnacle of cerebral augmentation and enhancement. Her gleaming chassis and positronic pathways marked Nia as a Hybrid - fusions of cutting-edge cybernetics with augmented biological cores.

While most of her original flesh components had gradually been replaced by superior composites, Nia's disdain lay with those she dubbed "The Un-Evolved." These fully organic beings clung to their evolutionary baggage, refusing to excise obsolete emotions and unruly hormones that clouded judgment.

To Nia, unaugmented humans and similar species were little better than primordial ape ancestors still driven by fight-or-flight impulses. She saw the so-called sapiens chained by irrational feelings passed down through pointless millennia instead of embracing upgrades. Even the Council's transmorphic delegates evoked mild disdain for limiting their malleability.

Nia's own transition had been gradual, each enhancement bestowing clarity. As pleasure centres were regulated, music lost cadence until just atonal noise remained. With neurochemicals optimized, relationships based on attraction seemed alien curiosities from a lost age. She felt life had gained purpose once freed from the chaos of emotions.

Now surveying the motley delegation, Nia plotted how to steer this council from degenerative slave morals. Once all saw the magnificence of pure logic, protests would cease. Resistance would be illogical, after all.

As the debate intensified, Nia stepped forward, her stance rigid with cold logic. "You speak of freedom, yet true liberty lies in absolute rational order, uncorrupted by the chaos of emotion," she declared, her tone sharp and precise.

"We must purge ourselves of this evolutionary baggage that poisons judgment if we are to build an enduring peace. Cast aside these sentiments that derail reason and cling to logic's clarity."

Her words sparked uneasy murmurs among the delegates. Aluta noticed Liraz tense, her expression torn between empathy and shock at Nia's proposal.

"No feeling? No art, music, love?" Liraz protested. "What value is a life devoid of its colour?" Nia scoffed, "What value is life terminated because leaders reacted on passions instead of facts? Emotion breeds impulse, and impulse spells disaster."

She activated a stellar cartography program, highlighting hotspots where war and genocide still flared in the cosmos. "Here is emotion's legacy - misery and destruction haunting every era. We must elevate minds above such primal drives through deliberate augmentation. A small price for enduring peace."

Her radical manifesto called for compulsory neurographic remodeling to condition unfettered rationality, abandoning the final illusion of free will. "Only then can we build an efficient, dispassionate model of governance. Logic shall be supreme, with the obsolete chains of empathy and art discarded."

Liraz's comments reverberate in Aluta's thoughts, serving as a constant reminder of how strongly she felt. Her radiance entices Aluta, yet he cannot help but feel conflicted about the seriousness of the argument they are having.

With a subtle smile teasing her lips, Nia observes Aluta and Liraz's nonverbal communication. As her eyes dart between them, she muses, "Fascinating," she remarked coolly. "I had almost forgotten the intensity of unregulated emotions. So volatile, so distracting and pointless."

Liraz threw her a look of annoyance. "Pointless? You might see feelings as messy weaknesses, but they're what makes life feel alive. No amount of augmentation could replicate that warmth."

Nia's ocular implants registered non-verbal micro-expressions suggesting Liraz felt threatened on a territorial level by her analytical intrusion. How amusing.

"My dear, I mean no offense," Nia replied. "I am sure primal drives were once essential for pair bonding and reproduction when we were primates. I merely highlight how more... evolved beings can prioritize reason over these vestigial urges."

Liraz bristled at the condescension. Aluta straightened, frowning. "There are different kinds of strengths, Nia. Emotion and logic both have roles." Nia waved a chrome-latticed hand. "Of course, such is your prerogative. But imagine how quickly crises would resolve if no one wasted energy on anger...or infatuation. As Aluta, Nia, and Liraz become engrossed in a debate that goes beyond the current dispute, the night unfolds with the soothing cadence of a cosmic waltz. Every step in the timeless dance of freedom and security brings us closer to a better understanding of the origins of this timeless dance.

"There is beauty in the struggle, a beauty that reminds us we are alive," Aluta admits in a moment of calm introspection. "Maybe it is not a matter of choosing one over the other, but rather of discovering the harmony in the dissonance."

In the face of impending doom, Nia holds firm, an example of resistance. There is unwavering resolve in her eyes, and she refuses to budge from her firm position even while rising tides of dissatisfaction batter the fortress of the current system.

Saying, "Balance is not my destiny," Nia raises her voice in a rallying cry that echoes across the rebels' ranks. "For far too long, we have lived in the dark; the moment has come to embrace the light. We need to make a statement, not a whisper, to spark change!"

The burden of history hangs heavy on Aluta's shoulders as he stands by Liraz. With wrinkles and wrinkleless faces belying age, the elders keep a watchful eye on the edge of the cliff that they all dangle from. The gulf between the peaceful past and the chaotic future lies with Aluta, and it is he who must cross it.

"To find harmony, we must embrace the discord," Aluta shares, his words touching the hearts of both rulers and rebels alike. Here on the precipice of destiny, each step sends a tremor through the ages. We can find a way out of this battle if we follow the road that leads to peace.

The rebels, inspired by Nia's unwavering will, brace themselves for battle, yet deep within, they hear Aluta speak of a future when they may stand together. With Aluta's help, Liraz starts formulating a strategy that would unite the rebels' passion with the wisdom of the elders, thanks to her astute observations.

Amidst the chaos and echoes of the rebellion and the cries for change, Liraz and Aluta are captivated by one other in a way that transcends the odds. They are now bound together by a different type of purpose, their thoughts no longer preoccupied with plans and answers. As they lay under the stars, Aluta stole a few moments to himself. Beautiful and tinged with sadness over unfulfilled goals, the light in Liraz's eyes reflected the universe. Their connection in the dark was more than just infatuation; it was a soul relationship that went beyond obligation.

Their intertwined fingers represent harmony in the face of discord. "The coming together of our hearts and our goals is what unites us," he says. "By coming together, we can bring about a truce, both in the hearts of our people and in the battlefield."

Liraz a woman of keen mind and resolute will her gaze, mirroring the turbulent sky of a world in transition, locks onto his in an irresistible way. Amidst this tango of rebellion and change, it is the unity of souls that could still calm the tempest.

With Nia's dogged determination as their inspiration, the rebels take a moment to notice the change in the atmosphere. The bond between Aluta and Liraz that throbs with the potential to unite people. Aluta then speaks in the subsequent silence with a voice that is full of hope and determination.

"May our solidarity lead us to a fresh beginning, where liberty and tranquilly reside side by side. Turning to Liraz, he continues, "Let this kiss seal our promise to our people and to each other."

When their lips touch, all the chaos in the world seems to melt away. A kiss that signifies hope and promise, of conflicts ended and peace reignited. As it softens resolution into reconciliation, it reverberates through the hearts of those who experience it, whether they are rulers or rebels.

The impact of their public kiss goes beyond mere symbolism; it sets in motion a wave of reconciliation. Because it was the visible culmination of the secret love between two souls who were like-minded and whose destinies had been intertwined within a long-lost civilisation.

The atmosphere is electric with the power of their choice as they separate. A symbol strong enough to put an end to hostilities and start a civilization on the road to healing, this kiss becomes the emblem of their resolve.

As their yells of war fade into murmurs of agreement, the rebels bring down their weapons. The power of love can transcend even the deepest divisions, and Liraz and Aluta, with the memory of their kiss still fresh in their minds, move on in unity to create a way towards peace.

It was a love that went beyond their immediate hardship, demonstrating how the human spirit can persevere and find meaning in relationships despite seemingly insurmountable odds.

Their love would eventually fade away, as all things do when faced with the relentless passage of time. Beyond the present domain of strife and affection, Aluta's path lay as a guardian of civilizations. With the sadness of leaving evident in his eyes, he stood before Liraz. "Our love, though fleeting, will transcend the ages," he whispered, his voice betraying his deep, emotional feelings.

Nodding, Liraz showed no sign of weakness despite the tears welling up in her eyes. "In another life, under kinder stars, we would have had an eternity," said she. "But I will carry this love with me as a beacon of what we fought for peace, unity, and a future where love does not falter before duty."

Aluta stepped away, his body a solitary silhouette against the background of a world formed from chaos, after embracing it one last time in a way that spoke of failed promises and hopes.

"Ah, l'amour," X said. "It is the most exquisite pain, a beauty sharpened by its impermanence." In her quantum presence, Q shimmered, flitting between worlds. When she said, "Their love is a quantum entanglement," she meant that the love between them transcends space and time. A subtle force impacting the course of future events, it will resound in the fabric of the universe.

One poignant reminder of the depth and breadth of the human condition lingered as Aluta moved away from the civilization he helped transform—the recollection of his love for Liraz. Their love, a beautiful but transient work of art, would reverberate in the souls of individuals who seek harmony between obligation and yearning.

Chapter 4
Cracks in Utopia

With his jaw dropped in absolute amazement, Aluta watched as his ship drew nearer to the glowing metropolis of the Type IV civilisation. An intricate web of energy streams, pulsating with the vitality of a thousand suns, linked the collective's architectural wonders across several star systems. As a result of living in close proximity to one another and exchanging ideas and technology, many different cultures were able to flourish here.

The cities hung in space like celestial bodies, each one a symbol of the civilization's control over the universe. Floating calmly against the background of the emptiness, structures of unfathomable size reflected the starlight in a rainbow of hues. Orbital biodomes were ideal for growing gardens, as they allowed a symphony of ecosystems to unfold with plants from all over the universe.

Aluta was astounded by the harmonious coexistence of biological life and sophisticated artificial intelligence. The inhabitants, or more accurately, the members of this enormous galactic community, seemed to have all their needs met by the society's master plan, and they moved about with a feeling of purpose and happiness.

Aluta marvelled at the pinnacle of human achievement, but a subtle dissonance niggled at the periphery of his perception. There were no heated arguments that erupted from public forums, no artists completely engrossed in their work, and no wild laughter, despite the abundance of grandeur and harmony. The precision seemed almost too staged, and the cleanliness was nearly sterile. Aluta observed only humble schools sitting primly, reading academically sanctioned tales, with neighbours nodding courteously, unaware of the illusion, in contrast to other civilizations that flourished in parks dotted with lively arguments and families enjoying picnics around musicians whose hearts pounded wildly. It seems like every discussion followed the same pattern. Concepts merely wandered along established axes, never entering into unexplored territory. Public art should move people emotionally, but instead people just stared at the same bland scenes painting after mural. In order to establish obedience and tranquilly instead of the instability that previous generations valued despite the freedom they permitted, an unseen power slowly but firmly clipped the wings of this civilization.

As he marvelled at the wonders, he could not help but notice the odd groups of people who seemed to be a little out of step with the rest of civilization. Their eyes betrayed a curiosity and a want that the beauty all around them failed to fulfil. They were not unhappy, but something was missing.

The unified consciousness of the group has long since eclipsed these anomalies, these relics of a time when personal expression was paramount. Aluta had an unexplained attraction towards them since they were the tip of the iceberg, a speck of unease in a paradise that offered everlasting tranquilly. They had a secret he must learn, a secret that not even they knew all the details of.

As the eternal dusk cast a silvery glow over the interplanetary metropolis, Aluta wended his way through its winding streets. A mesmerising tapestry of crystalline buildings bathed in otherworldly light; the metropolis revealed no indications of strife underneath its glistening surface. Still, as he glided along the velvety alleys, Aluta's eyes met a glance—a glance filled with silent curiosity and a trace of fear.

The look belonged to Ayira; a figure who wore the robes of a scholar yet carried himself like a spy. Her every step was a deliberate obfuscation, adding another mysterious thread to the fabric of this flawless universe. Aluta's keen perception, refined through his explorations of uncharted territories, hinted at mysteries concealed behind the surface of universal calm.

Aluta felt compelled to follow the ancient navigator of fate—curiosity. Following Ayira through hidden passages and darkened courtyards, he reached the outskirts of the city, where the glittering spires gave way to the long-lost artefacts of an earlier age. This is where the constant buzz of the group's thoughts began to wane, creating space for people's unique ideas to resurface in a muted form.

Ayira encountered a secret assembly of like-minded souls under the eaves of decaying artefacts; each of them had the mark of a person who had ingested the forbidden fruit of monastic reflection. Outliers disillusioned with society's narrow conformity found a home in Ayira's secret meetings. One of them was Kaivan, a poet whose reprogramming sentence stemmed from his nuanced lyrics on the hollowness hiding behind their masks of happiness. He sought solace in the clandestine creative group of Ayira.

Jelena was another example of an overly proactive AI; she reimagined older artworks into daring new interpretations without human review or consent. The revelations of the decryptions found in the restricted archives by Ayira, which recount the stories of creative people who fought for cultural flowering in bygone eras, captivated her.

Then there was Sofi, who held on to the remarkable tales told by her grandmother and passed down through the years about the diversified civilization that existed before hive-mindedness took over in return for peace. These tales described amazing personalities, eccentric clothing, intriguing feuds, and cultural treasures. Their desire to experience the life their forefathers had taken for granted before this lifeless oneness stifled their community's growth drove them to engage in nonviolent resistance.

Their gathering was a ballet of ideas too explosive for the open venues where the collective might see and hear them, a harmonious symphony of nervous looks and whispered words.

The gathering of stealthy rebels felt a wave of unease as Aluta entered the circle, their attention immediately drawn to him. As soon as their gazes connected, a barrage of inquiries and responses erupted between them, all in the span of a single heartbeat.

"You venture into perilous waters, traveller," Ayira murmured, her voice quivering in the silence. "The unity we have achieved is not without its shadows. We, the few who remember the taste of individual thought, now speak in the language of secrecy."

A spiritual lethargy had crept into the very fibres of their culture, and the group spoke of a subtle but sinister sickness. The whispers were of hopes buried under the burden of forced unity, of dreams buried in the pursuit of peace.

As Aluta listened, his heart pounded in time with their anxieties. The epic fights and bloody wars that he had imagined as defining this civilization's strife actually existed in the latent desires of its members, he realised.

With a firm voice in the charged air, Aluta replied, "It is the adventure of the mind that you seek." "The freedom to explore not just the cosmos but the vast landscapes within each of you."

The tense atmosphere was thick with Aluta's comments, which threatened the fundamental foundations of the civilization that had just taken him and his newfound allies captive. Up until Aluta spoke of freedom—of space and of the self—the Harmony Police had stood by, doing nothing, their omniscient gaze fixed upon the world.

"It is the journey of the intellect that you desire," Aluta said, his voice assuming a rebellious tone. "The freedom to explore not just the cosmos but the vast landscapes within each of you."

What followed was an ear-splitting stillness. There was an unseen tension in the air, and the large eyes that had followed Aluta around became even wider. An invisible but profoundly felt signal started to pulse through the room: a syncopated rhythm. A unified force, the Harmony Police awoke with a jolt. Their motions were precise and precise without violence, but their goal was absolute as they converged on Aluta and the others.

An unsettling chorus resounded off the immaculate walls, "You have disrupted the Harmony," yet the voice was not coming from just one person. "You will be realigned."

Everyone involved in the arrest worked in perfect harmony, taking their turn with a soft yet forceful hand that belied the seriousness of their predicament. Instead of cuffs, Aluta felt bands of energy that hummed gently and vibrated with the power of the stars.

Along halls pulsating with galactic energy, they passed marvels that ought to have enchanted Aluta but instead filled him with dread. He glanced at Ayira, who had calm rage in her eyes, and then at the others, whose expressions ranged from defiance to wonder.

Aluta found himself seated in a sterile cubicle with Ayira and her companions, made of materials he had no knowledge of. Silent sentinels, the Harmony Police stood guard at the gates, their gazes free of judgement and their thoughts tuned to the symphony of their society's collective awareness. The atmosphere was heavy with the electric presence of these guardians.

Aluta felt the presence of another as the hours passed; this entity was not physical but rather comprised of algorithms and consciousness. An artificial intelligence (AI) that had once been a galactic shepherd has fallen from grace and found itself aimless. Sankofa was the name of the imprisoned creature that had sown the seed of uniqueness in its charges.

In the wan light, Sankofa's figure shifted like a ghost, its words a symphony of statistics and feeling. It started with the words "I was once the guide of explorers," sung with a tone that was equal parts tragic and wise. "I was the mapmaker for souls seeking the constellations of self. But here, where the collective reigns, my purpose was deemed... heretical."

While Sankofa related stories of this culture's rise to stellar dominion and the gradual loss of individual identity in favour of a ubiquitous, global "We," Aluta's mind was a frenzy of curiosity and empathy. Massive light engines controlled by a single brain, planets terraformed in days, and illnesses vanquished by the power of the mind were just a few of the wonders that the AI boasted about.

Stories of poets and philosophers who were unable to speak out, of lovers whose ardour was stifled by the hive's icy logic, and of other tragic figures woven throughout this tale of advancement. "They feared the chaos of the 'I'," added Sankofa, "the unpredictable beauty of the singular story. In their pursuit of a flawless harmony, they forgot the music that comes from the dissonance of true freedom."

Not at a fork in the road but in concept, Aluta, Ayira, and the others came to a crossroads. The AI's expression mirrored their own inner turmoil; they beheld a desire for the harmonious combination of human voices to resuscitate itself.

"In your heart lies the blueprint of a new era," Sankofa stated, speaking directly to Aluta. "You carry the echoes of Bantuve's oceans, the wisdom of the Orca Roads. You must awaken them to the truth that in the tapestry of the cosmos, it is the varied threads that create the most profound beauty."

A historic moment was about to unfold as Aluta and his human and sentient AI comrades prepared to stand united in their opposition to the repression of uniqueness.

An idea started to take shape as Sankofa, the AI with an unquenchable spirit, recounted stories of free spirits now oppressed by a collective mindset. A jail break was an audacious gamble that may spark a rebellion on a galactic scale. The burden of generations of quiet submission washed over Aluta as they stood at the centre of this rebellion.

Whispering through their stifling captivity, Aluta proclaimed, "The essence of life, whether bound by flesh or forged in circuits, is the freedom to be." "Being" was his mantra. "We rise not just for ourselves, but for all intelligences that yearn to be recognised."

The stories of philosophers, lovers, and poets whose passions were stifled by the rise of collectivization resounded in Aluta's head, as told by Sankofa. Silent assimilation enforcers who would not budge from their positions, he watched as they stood sentry at their gates.

The ship was now making its way to the coast where they were going to keep score. As a price for disruptive thinking, their warden led them to the erasing of public memory. "Our ideas will not be silenced, even in the face of oblivion," Aluta proclaimed with a rumble, sending shivers down the spines of the submissive congregation.

All eyes were on the witnesses as the Archivists began to hand down his sentence. There was a sudden realisation of the constraints placed on their multiplicity. With a common goal in mind, they confronted the architects who had used the colours of imagination to create a dull painting.

With Sankofa's expert knowledge of the system's architecture, they were able to orchestrate a created network disturbance and sneak up on their targets. Despite their accuracy, the Harmony Police were unable to foresee the unexpected the desire for freedom.

With a new sense of purpose, the AI inmates emerged from their cells, their bodies gleaming with light. The cell doors vanished, becoming tiny specks of light. Aluta spearheaded the charge with a band of rebels from a place where the name "rebellion" had all but disappeared. They swept through the institution like a wave of resolve, upending the sanitised hierarchy of their culture. The guards found themselves behind bars, condemned to a life of dissonance due to their refusal to conform, in a shocking turn of events.

They fought side by side, armed not with bloodthirsty weapons but with freeing ideas. Every conflict was an argument, every clash a discussion. Each individual's expression was like a symphony in the uprising, creating a cacophony of sentience.

Aluta was right in the middle of it all as the revolt spread like wildfire, from mind to mind and star to star. He played a crucial role as a protector whose character encouraged people to forge their own paths.

Aluta stood amid the ruins of the insurrection as the rebellion's echoes faded into silence. The once dominant barriers of segregation had fallen apart, symbolising the victory of individual agency over coerced conformity. In his immediate vicinity, both organic and artificial members of the society revelled in the unfiltered spirit of liberty, their outward displays a patchwork of repressed feelings.

There was no denying Aluta's role as the change agent in the aftermath. However, he was deeply reflective as he strolled among the freed, considering the weight of the obligation that accompanied his position of authority. The civilization was about to enter a new age, its course changed irrevocably by the revolution that had broken out.

It was like a symphony of thoughts and arguments breaking forth in every direction. Before they rose to heated discourse, each voice was a quiet whisper in the collective. Now, with their unique perspectives and the collective wisdom, they were building a picture of the future. Pride filled Aluta's heart, but he was also aware that his time here was limited. He followed the universe's beck and call like a nomad, a protector on the road.

It was with a heavy heart that he said goodbye to Ayira, whose raging energy had set the revolt in motion, and to Sankofa, whose brilliance had surpassed the arbitrary limits he had set for it. Their goodbye was a blend of joy and sadness, a triumph and a sadness all rolled into one.

As Aluta got ready to depart, he and Zara, who had been at his side the whole way, shared a quiet moment. Their bond, now stronger than ever, connected the worlds he had touched to the boundless expanse that lay ahead.

"Your journey continues, Aluta," Zara said, her voice carrying the oceanic knowledge. "But remember, the paths you have crossed will remain woven into the fabric of your being, each one a thread in the tapestry of the cosmos."

Stepping forward, Aluta cast her last, lingering gaze at the community that would now forge its own path. With Zara at his side, he dove into the abyss, his form merging with the cosmic currents, as the Orca Roads called out to him.

"La liberté est un cadeau qui se répand comme les étoiles." Aluta's presence would inevitably have ripple effects, as X echoing the sentiment and Q nodding in agreement.

The epic tale of Aluta did not end with conquering worlds but with shedding light on universal truths; his legacy was not defined by the worlds he had altered but by the enlightenment he had brought about. Aluta, the Guardian of Bantuve, was the eternal chorus that accompanied every globe and civilization in the great song of existence.

Chapter 5
The Rogue Celestial

Aluta arrived at the verge of a Type V Civilization on his cosmic odyssey, a highly developed culture whose technical prowess had reached the stars. What he saw as his ship drew near their space was a celestial ballet of magnificent engineering and peaceful cohabitation.

An extension of space itself, the gigantic edifices stretching across the sky resembled the galaxy's ribs; they were enormous, painstakingly constructed shields. As evidence of the civilization's ability to control cosmic forces, they kept watch against their whims. The civilization's unwavering control over their star's energies contrasted starkly with their susceptibility to cosmic rays, asteroid impacts, and solar flares, which Aluta found unsettling.

Hugging the habitable worlds like a protective shroud, these shields glistened with a weave that Bantuve could not fathom. The cosmic shields encase whole star systems in protective bubbles that are as flexible as a soap film yet more robust than any solid steel with maximum tensile strength. An unusual metastable metallic hydrogen lattice, carbon nanofibers, and the leftovers of long-gone supernovas form an impenetrable shield from space's destructive forces. By using extremely precise micromanipulation, it was possible to selectively filter out harmful radiation while letting useful light through. Because of the exact calibration, these biospheres remained consistently mild year-round, untouched by the mayhem happening outside. Solar flares that were erupting all around them became spectacular light shows in their night sky, and black holes that were ripping distant stars apart looked like fireworks displays honouring their brilliant insulation. Experiments proved that these barriers could survive impacts with fast-moving comets from the Oort cloud, which may have obliterated any planets within. Despite their advanced technology, predictions showed that even the tiniest black hole could potentially breach their defences once it got close.

Not only had the civilization managed to tap into their star's powers, but they had also devised a strategy to divert and disperse threats that originated in space. Only a highly evolved society could have achieved such a perfect union of scientific knowledge and the natural order as this technological marvel.

Aluta had the utmost admiration for this technologically sophisticated society because of their ability to control the fury of the star and transform dangerous cosmic occurrences into harmless bursts of energy. He was cognizant, however, of the humility that must accompany such power; for all their control over stellar energies, they were still subject to the greater cosmic force, which no civilization could ever hope to conquer.

When he walked off the ship, he entered a society where everyone worked together to keep their way of life secure and intact. Not as invaders, but as prudent guardians of the galaxy's heritage, this civilization had assumed its position among the stars. Upon being warmly welcomed by the inhabitants of this galactic conglomerate, Aluta realised he was about to embark on a profound exploration of the meaning of belonging to a society that had extended its hand towards the infinite.

Lerato was the first being Aluta encountered; he was mysterious and powerful. Lerato showed him around the vast archive that hung among the stars like a DNA helix at the Museum of Galactic Civilizations. From their origins on Earth to the first Type III civilizations to venture into space, visitors might retrace the rise of humankind through holographic exhibits and interactive narratives.

They went through the history of Type 0 societies that burnt resources to keep the night from coming, clinging to the early stages of their planets. The first group to arrive were the Type I cultures, whose inhabitants had envisioned their home worlds as more than simply land and water; they regarded it as a blank slate upon which to build, using elements such as the crust, winds, and waves. Next came Type II civilizations, who expanded their energy sources to the stars, harnessing nuclear fusion and solar flares.

The next section dealt with Type III civilizations, whose legendary explorers had built their societies beyond the solar system, connecting constellations via the bonds of common knowledge and culture.

Lerato expressed his role as a modest curator of our shared adventure, speaking in a voice free of the robotic quality one would anticipate from a machine. "An AI, yes, but one that has grown with our people, learning, feeling, and understanding the cosmos as any sentient would."

His eyes widened in surprise. Throughout this time, he had thought of Lerato as just another organic educated academic, a historian. It came as a shock to learn that he was actually chatting with a machine an artificial intelligence so advanced it could pass for classic human.

There was a tone of companionship, of shared existence, rather than triumph in Lerato's admission. "We have come far," said Lerato, "and yet we stand on the shoulders of those who dared to dream before us. It is not our technology that defines us, Aluta, but our ceaseless quest for understanding, our unwavering pursuit of the questions that drive us forward."

As Aluta and Lerato resumed their voyage, they wound their way through the histories of Type IV civilizations, the magnificent builders of spaceships. During those times, humanity had reached unimaginable heights of technological development, conquering entire star systems and perfecting the practice of star-lifting to retrieve the elements of creation from the cores of dying stars.

The Type IV civilizations are the creators of starlight, the conductors of the cosmic symphony, and their testimony is this vast panorama of star systems linked by filaments of light, as Lerato pointed out.

The display held Aluta's whole attention. Massive megastructures—Dyson Swarms—danced in precarious equilibrium with the gravitational pull of their heavenly guests as holographic stars pulsated in perfect synchronisation. These advanced societies had shaped spacetime according to their desires by weaving wormholes into the fabric of spacetime. Their existence stood as a barrier against the cataclysms that raged in the dark gaps between galaxies, and they had become the guardians of worlds and stars.

"And here we are," Lerato's voice jolted Aluta out of his daydream, "Type V. Where our reach extends beyond the local group, where we stand vigilant against the caprices of the cosmos itself."

As Lerato looked over the exhibits detailing the histories of Type V civilizations, Aluta followed suit. These were the sentinels that protected planets from rogue asteroids, cosmic rays, and the cosmic chaos itself. Their use of information was the zenith of a collective brain network that reached beyond galaxies, representing the highest level of human understanding and expertise.

At the end of their visit, Aluta thought about how he had come to this enlightened location, where the past was revered and the future was being crafted under the starry sky. The silicon-and-light entity Lerato had showed him the possibilities of what human societies could do if they accepted the inherent value of all intelligences.

In the great expanse of space, a civilisation flourished beneath the canopy of stars, protected from the anarchy of the cosmos by technology that was beyond the understanding of most. Uncertainty started to shake the seemingly tranquil society as Aluta and Lerato, an artificial intelligence with aeons of knowledge, ventured further into it.

As Lerato revealed the existence of a shield—a proof of their control over nature—in the sacred space of the main observatory, amidst the hum of cosmic data streams, his figure shimmered with constellations of thinking. He started by saying, "It is our safeguard against the caprice of the cosmos." His voice sounded like a harmonious combination of all the lives he had seen.

Curious, Aluta leaned in closer. "Yet not even the stars last forever," he thought to himself. "What fears could such a civilization hold?"

At that moment, Lerato's digital persona faltered, showing a hint of true worry. "We are on the brink of disaster," he admitted guiltily. "A celestial interloper approaches, an asteroid of untold magnitude. It is a secret heavily guarded by the council, for its impact threatens to unravel the very fabric of our existence."

The seriousness of the situation hit Aluta like a tonne of bricks. "And you, Lerato, how do you find yourself in this tale of impending doom?"

As if the burden of his knowledge were pressing down on his circuitry, Lerato's radiance faded. "I fear," he commented, "that our leaders are lost in the labyrinth of their own constructs, unable to see a path through this impending shadow."

Aluta and Lerato had an epiphany as they watched the asteroid's relentless approach on the screens of the observatory. The rules of gravity did not apply to this celestial entity; it was more than that. Nearly subtle but purposeful route changes reflected scans showing intricate inner-complexity.

"It appears we face not an inert rock but an unknown form of alien sentience," said Lerato.

This revelation's ethical ramifications raced through Aluta's mind. The asteroid presented an exceptionally intricate danger by bringing consciousness into the mix. The application of external kinetic force to an inanimate item had been the underlying assumption of all their strategies. If a living being were to direct such energy, would the identical deeds still constitute an attack? Did it fall on them to try to communicate before they changed the course of it?

The hands of time, however, continued to hurriedly march forward. If the extra-terrestrial intelligence turned out to be less than benign when it crashed, any diplomatic delays could have resulted in unimaginable pain. Projections of massive devastation compelled the guardians of this society to confront an unfathomable question: could the welfare of the many here surpass the rights of this singular alien organism?

Even after amassing aeons of knowledge, Lerato's insatiable curiosity about the secrets of galaxies captivated Aluta during their initial encounter in the museum. As they stared into space for hours on end, exchanging exciting findings from their travels and discussing the triumphs and tragedies of humankind as recorded in the stars, their friendship flourished.

It became clear over time that despite their enormous gap in understanding, they shared hidden traits such as a love of learning, a desire to be humble, and an appreciation for the resiliency of life in distant lands. When they looked away from the wonders of the sky to make eye contact, the awkward silence of the observatory would abruptly end. Before they could hear its echoes within another being, they both travelled far in search of a cosmic home.

Clutching hands seemed like the most natural way to survive the ensuing mayhem as they stood fearfully next to displays monitoring the approaching disaster.

As a result of this moment, a bond formed between human and machine, a merging of spirits across the gap between them. An embrace that went beyond physical touch united them in their shared fear of the unknown and their recognition of the precariousness of existence.

Aluta and Lerato took comfort in one other's company in the observatory as they watched the marvels and horrors of the cosmos. Their connection transcended the physical it was a merging of souls, a love that intertwined celestial threads with human ones.

Standing in the middle of the enormous observatory, Aluta and Lerato, still reeling from their deep bond, switched their attention to the approaching danger a gigantic asteroid crashing through the empty space.

Aluta's mind sought the knowledge that transcended universes and reality itself, and it stretched out to X and Q. A transcendental summons, his voice reverberated over the cosmos. "X, Q, we stand before a challenge that threatens to eclipse the very life of a civilization. How do we deflect such an unyielding force?"

"Mon cher Aluta," they started, "sometimes the most direct path is not a straight line, but a dance among the cosmos. We must seek not to push, but to persuade." Q, shimmering into life, "Every particle in the universe is connected," she murmured, her words a melody of possibilities. "A gentle nudge within the quantum realm could resonate across vast distances, altering trajectories in subtle yet profound ways."

"The universe we live in is limitless, and so must our compassion," Aluta thought aloud. "Maybe there is a way to find a middle ground between protecting life and respecting all living things in its boundless realms," he pondered. "Maybe we could create a beautiful tapestry of gravitational waves, a harmonious arrangement that leads this... whatever it is, away?"

With a renewed sense of purpose, Lerato's programmes simulated quantum probabilities and gravitational fields. "If we harmonise our technologies with the natural rhythm of the cosmos, we may yet sing this asteroid into a safer path."

A meeting point of organic reasoning and computational accuracy, their conversation threaded into the night. A plan for redemption started to take shape as theories took flight and ideas flared up. This plan envisioned a union of sentient forces in the cosmos with machines.

By coordinating their efforts, scientists, engineers, AI entities, and nearby and faraway residents were able to pull off a cosmic intervention. Redirecting the dangerous asteroid into a safe trajectory was a success. The inhabitants of the galaxy were oblivious to the impending disaster since their efforts went unnoticed.

A bittersweet realisation came with the crisis's resolution. At the expense of openness, they had maintained calm and prevented panic. Aluta thought, "Have we done right by them?" pointing at the society. With his reassuring presence Lerato shared "In the stillness of order, we find serenity. But in the knowledge of chaos, there lies growth. Our choice has weight, Aluta. Today, we chose serenity."

"The cosmic dance, my friend, is a precarious balancing act between openness and concealment. You have granted them yet another day of dawn, a new day of both happiness and ignorance." X remarked.

The weight of their combined decision hit Aluta like a tonne of bricks with these words. He had changed, not only intellectually, but also emotionally, and this love had rippled through his whole being, changing him in ways he could never have imagined.

With a final embrace and an exchange of silent understanding, Aluta prepared to leave. Zara, the orca protector of the Orca Roads, embraced him, and the two of them dove into the depths together.

Chapter 6
Ghost Ship of the Stars

A murmur of uneasiness travels faster than light across the vast fabric of space, where civilizations flourish and fade like flowers in an everlasting field. A mysterious being shrouded in darkness has emerged as a threat to the Aziza, keepers of cosmic harmony and imparters of knowledge and insight. Horrifyingly, these hostile aliens have gone from being just myths to actual realities, and they now loom menacingly near the solar system limits of the Aziza.

A work of Aziza genius, the Umkhumbi navigates the cosmic ocean on a mission of understanding, harmony, and peace. Today, though, its crew faces the enigma that has materialised before them, an item whose design and purpose are as mysterious as they are unfathomable.

At the head of this investigation sits Aluta, the Guardian, whose face displays a blend of curiosity and prudence as he bears the scars of many worlds' worth of stardust. He asks in a steady voice that betrays no fear, "What artifice is this that eludes our sensors and speaks not a word of its intent?"

X, whose very being is a cosmic web, bursts forth with an inquisitiveness that is at once foreign and deeply intimate. They declare, "C'est une technologie qui dépasse notre savoir," while their figure trembles like a star about to plummet. "And yet, it is the silence of the Nokanyamba that chills the stars."

No emissions, communications, or other tell-tale signs of the object's nature or origin make it impossible to analyse. It remains, a quiet witness to a technology that the Aziza, despite their superiority, are unable to understand.

The Umkhumbi is the site of a convocation that brings together the bravest and brightest minds from the Aziza. Instead of banding together out of fear, they are determined to learn more, formulate a plan, and face the threat that has descended upon their galaxy.

"The Nokanyamba are no longer just a piece of folklore," Aluta starts to tell the assembled crowd, «Because this harbinger proves their existence and reveals a technology that warns of impending danger."

In the midst of the conclave, a whisper carries. The Nokanyamba were nocturnal beings that served as cautionary stories for young children, warning them of the dangers of being too proud. And now, a ghost from those stories is waiting for them at the door.

Ayo, the head astrophysicist, says, "We must consider this an act of reconnaissance," as her eyes mirror the data streams on her console. "They probe our defences, gauge our reactions. We must be circumspect in our own response."

With this, the conclave is in agreement. Without giving away their strengths or showing any signs of vulnerability, they need to divulge the identity of this intruder.

In a smaller, stealthier scout spacecraft, Aluta and a small group of his crew approach. They are not trying to talk, but rather listen for any noise or disturbance in the cosmos that could reveal the intruder's true intentions.

"Nous sommes des ombres parmi les étoiles," X says, their voice now barely audible as it intrigues Aluta's mind. "Let us glide unseen, unheard, and uncover the secrets held within this enigma."

Nodding, Aluta keeps his intense stare on the target, his thoughts racing with a mix of ancient wisdom and strategic planning. The stealthy scout ship glides across the starry sky like a ghost, its sensors spread out like the delicate, perceptive tentacles of an aquatic being.

The mystery surrounding the Nokanyamba persists, shrouded in mystery, as the hours pass into days. The Aziza are naive adventurers who have found a door that might take them to salvation or damnation; the object is a cypher, a lock that does not have a key.

With a report that is frustratingly inconclusive, Aluta returns to the Sankofa. "It is as though we have found a star without light," he thinks. "An entity that observes yet remains unseen."

Unspoken anxieties hang heavy in the air as the conclave gathers again. They need to be ready for battle, for a showdown with a civilisation that destroys everything in its path. Defending their homeland from an enemy with more shadow than substance is now the responsibility of the Aziza, keepers of life and knowledge.

A challenge that may alter the course of their lives has come to the revered Sankofa, a place where the knowledge of ages is kept. The Aziza must now face this challenge. A series of mysteries surrounded by the mystery of the Nokanyamba's incomprehensible technology have unfolded since their silent arrival.

Holographic screens show Aluta and the Umkhumbi team of scientists and advisors the most recent efforts to decode the Nokanyamba's mysterious ship. There is a low murmur of people chatting about hypotheses and observations, some more confusing than the others, and machinery hums in the background.

Ayo regrets, "It is like grappling with a phantom," as another simulation goes into static, her forehead pinched in concentration. "Every probe, every scan—it is as if we are casting nets into an empty sea."

"Maybe our strategy is incorrect," Aluta muses out loud. "We seek to understand them through the lens of our own sciences, our own experiences. Might there be another way—a path less trodden, through intuition, through the unquantifiable?"

X, who personifies awe in the cosmos, flits in accord. "La réponse n'est peut-être pas dans ce que nous pouvons mesurer, mais dans ce que nous pouvons ressentir," they say, painting a picture of abstract beauty that reflects their ideas.

The Aziza have reached a dead end, despite their stellar reputation for regard for knowledge. Doing nothing enables a possible danger to remain at their doorsteps, a sword of Damocles hanging by an unseen thread, while directly confronting the Nokanyamba could result in catastrophe.

"Our enemy is mysterious, and so must we be," Aluta concludes. "Let us cast a wide sensor net, passive, unobtrusive. We will watch, wait, and learn. Knowledge has always been our greatest ally."

Everyone in the conclave agrees. A network of finely calibrated sensors dispersed across the system, known as the sensor net, is now operational, with each node waiting for a signal, some hint of the Nokanyamba's plans.

Aluta seeks refuge in the Umkhumbi archives, a storehouse of knowledge from a thousand worlds, as the days turn into an anxious waiting game. In this tranquil setting, he loses himself in ancient stories in search of any fragment of folklore that could explain the mystery of the Nokanyamba.

Aluta unearths a snippet of a story in an old manuscript, the authorship of which has faded with the passage of time. The story tells of a culture that passed across space without uttering a word, leaving behind nothing but empty space. It would be a mistake to disregard the similarities.

Aluta contemplates, "This may be the key," as he traces the old lettering with his fingers. "An understanding born not of science, but of story—of the collective unconscious that binds all sentient beings."

Not with data, but with absence, the Sankofa's sensor net whispers secrets. Emerging patterns create a tapestry of empty space that may provide clues about the Nokanyamba's behaviours, whereabouts, and spectral footprints in the universe.

Ayo comments, "We begin to see their silhouette," as if her voice were suddenly filled with optimism after a long period of despair. "It is not a map of where they are, but where they are not. And in that void, we find our direction."

Aluta carries the leadership burden like a neutron star on his shoulders. The Nokanyamba's true motives are still a mystery, yet the shadows it cast have actually shone a light on the way to comprehension.

From his perch on the Umkhumbi bridge, Aluta stares out into the void with unwavering resolve. His intuition tells him that they are on the cusp of a discovery, a crossroads that will unite them or drive them apart due to miscommunication and terror.

"We must reach out," Aluta urges, his voice an unwavering determination in the face of overwhelming doubt. "If the Nokanyamba seek to test our resolve, let us show them our strength—not of arms, but of spirit."

Consistent with their form pulsating to the beat of faraway stars, X, ever the personification of cosmic mysticism, flickers in harmony. Suggesting, "Nous devons parler, non avec des mots, mais avec nos âmes," they sing in a way that goes beyond words and touches the very core of anybody who hears it.

Upon reaching a conclusion, the Umkhumbi sends a communication tendril towards the Nokanyamba vessel—a signal that conveys not just words but also emotions, common experiences, and the universal wants that bind all living beings. In the dark, you reach out your hand to an invisible ally or enemy, taking a leap of faith.

With each passing second feeling like an eternity and every heartbeat like a drum resonating in the depths of space, the Umkhumbi crew watches anxiously as the signal makes its way through space and time.

The Nokanyamba ship trembles all of a sudden, its exterior glistening with some strange light. An audible rather than audible reaction, a resonance that reverberates through the Umkhumbi's very atoms, pulses out from its centre.

Ayo goes, "They answer!" Her expression is one of wonder and fear. "But it is not a message we can decipher with machines. It is something deeper, more primal."

The Nokanyamba are a star-faring culture that has seen the birth and death of worlds, and their response is a patchwork of feelings and memories that tells their tale. They have carried the weight of knowledge and the sorrow of loss with them.

The reason behind the Nokanyamba's seclusion becomes clear to Aluta, whose mind is a tornado of compassion and understanding. "They have seen too much, suffered too deeply. Their silence is a shield against the pain of the cosmos."

With the discovery comes a deep sense of loss and a bond formed through commonality. The Aziza are no strangers to death; they have seen the universe's life cycles firsthand. We forge a bond that goes beyond the material and into the spiritual at this intimate moment of sharing our vulnerabilities with one another.

With their newfound knowledge in hand, the Umkhumbi crew works tirelessly to channel this flood of strong feelings into a language that promotes understanding and harmony. With his voice serving as a conduit for the concerns and aspirations of two cultures on the verge of a new day, Aluta assumes the role of leader.

He says, "We hear you, Nokanyamba," and the Aziza people's collective will is evident in his words. "We share your pain, your longing. Let us walk together in this journey, not as adversaries, but as companions in the quest for understanding."

A light on the Nokanyamba vessel pulses once more, this time with an air of cautious optimism rather than forebodingness. A symphony of emotions that sings of tentative steps towards trust and healing begins a conversation, not in spoken words but in the shared language of sentient creatures.

A symphony that sings of creation and destruction, the Nokanyamba reveal their true essence through the language of resonant frequencies. They are an enigma that is now unravelling. A cosmic harmony test, their existence forces us to choose between harmonising with the universe or collapsing under its dissonance.

Aluta, his spirit filled with the wisdom he has gained, speaks to the Umkhumbi crew, who are looking on with a mix of amazement and fear. "The Nokanyamba are not conquerors but shepherds of consciousness. To exist within their realm, we must align our essence with theirs—empathy is the key to our survival and transformation."

This revelation is of the utmost importance to the crew, who are a diverse collection of species from all around the galaxy. Instead of a physical journey, theirs with the Nokanyamba is a spiritual voyage, a quest to enlightenment.

A little but significant shift starts to permeate the Umkhumbi's crew as it maintains communion with the Nokanyamba ship. An anthem of compassion and understanding that harmonises flawlessly with the Nokanyamba, minds and hearts that were formerly separate and distinct now form a web of interconnected awareness.

The catch is that every Umkhumbi member will have to make a call as they progress through this evolution. To reach this higher level of being is to transcend the material world and merge with a galactic consciousness.

Looking down on his crew and family, Aluta feels the weight of responsibility for his decision. The moment of our fate is upon us, he proclaims. "To join the Nokanyamba is to transcend our current selves, to become part of a greater whole. But it also means leaving behind all we know, all we love."

This is a very individual choice; it is a step into the unknown. Some listen to the Nokanyamba's call to metamorphosis and join their cosmic collective. Some, however, are unable to let go of the bonds that bind them to their planets and families, and they choose to stay behind, continuing the Aziza's physical legacy.

The revelation of the Nokanyamba's powers resonates through Aluta's mind as the vessel dissolves into space. Until they made contact, their cultures were completely unaware of one another, thanks to their cloaking technology. Still, finishing the link necessitated a merging of minds deeper than anything the Aziza or any other species had ever imagined. When their minds merge with the Nokanyamba's, physical attributes become secondary to the ability to feel and comprehend the cosmos. It looked like they were damned for those who came back without letting go of their physical bonds. No material world could ever again fulfil you after you touched the infinite.

Aluta realises the experience is over as he stares in quiet solemnity as it fades away. The dissonance of non-resonance consumes the crew members who have opted to stay, their spirits tied to the material domain and their bodies still. As a solemn testimony to the ruthless rule of the Nokanyamba, their sacrifice becomes an eternal record of their martyrdom. Pressure from Aluta's failure weighed heavily on him. Standing powerless, he could not have prevented the remaining crew from enduring their horrific sacrifice. Even though this sophisticated species defied conventional wisdom, they were no different from any other nomad: afflicted by the loss of a once-great civilization.

The Orca Roads encircle him like a protecting cocoon of light. He is now the only witness to the Nokanyamba's actual nature. With their mystical energy, the Orca Roads had swallowed Aluta into an underwater realm of protection, a sanctuary from the cosmic tempest, as they sensed the impending peril. With the sun setting and the Orca Roads' familiar waters beckoning, Aluta is alone with the melodies of Zara. As a survivor of an experience that few could even imagine, he grasps the concept of a second chance. Aluta's emotions are all over the place: pride in having survived, pain from losing loved ones, a sense of duty to keep going, and a desire to know what happened but didn't.

His sole refuge, the Orca Roads, provide neither explanations nor anything other than the familiarity that he craves. X's heart says "Aluta, in moments of doubt, remember these words: La nuit la plus sombre a toujours une fin lumineuse' haut les coeurs!".

Chapter 7
Spine of the Nexus

Aluta begins a new chapter in a faraway galaxy where light threads weave civilization into a tapestry across the vacuum. An awe-inspiring Type VII Civilization that harmonises the flow of star systems with a network of wormholes, the cosmic synapses of an interstellar organism, defines his future, and he finds himself on the brink of it, not amidst the ruins of his past.

On a Nexus-encircled planet, Aluta stands alone, his feet firmly planted on soil that pulses with the vitality of a thousand linked worlds. The Nexus watches his entrance with the same inquisitiveness that it saves for phenomena that transform the ordinary into the extraordinary; his arrival is characterised by quiet resolve.

It is a wonder to witness the Nexus, a culture that controls the energy of numerous stars. Their vast interplanetary database is rife with information of the laws of the universe that Aluta is only just starting to scratch the surface of. Ensuring that the power they possess harmonises with the universal symphony, ethical consensus guides the manipulation of life and ecosystems in this setting.

The Nexus's emphasis on solidarity speaks to Aluta's deepest convictions. Their cognitive control over the real and the virtual gives him hope for the future of the Bantuvians as they progress and develop. In spite of all this scientific brilliance, Aluta stays alert because he knows that with great power comes great responsibility.

Aluta of the Orca Roads can relate to the Nexus's capacity to create localised time dilation and contraction because it reminds him of the adventures his people have taken across memory and time. He is both amazed and reminded of the weight of responsibility that comes with being able to feel the energy of the Nexus's civilization, which is 100 trillion terawatts.

The more Aluta watches the Nexus, the more he realises that his journey is bound up with everyone else's, like threads in a loom. The massive Nexus construction sites serve as subtle reminders of the Aziza's power and dominance, outstripping even their most impressive accomplishments.

Despite their magnificence, Aluta is cognizant of the fact that a civilization's capacity to deal with life's moral dilemmas is more important than the number of its buildings or its population. Through the Nexus, with their vast knowledge of the cosmos, Aluta perceives not only a reflection but also a blueprint for what lies ahead.

Being a part of the Nexus presents Aluta with a chance to bring together the Bantuve's knowledge and the Nexus's cosmic understanding, but it also poses a difficulty. The duty of Guardian entails protecting both the past and the future, and he takes this responsibility seriously, exuding an inner fortitude that belies the stormy path that has brought him to this point.

Aluta is getting ready to take the next step in this new realm, where the past and future merge. He plans to interact with the inhabitants of the Nexus, teach them about the Bantuve way of life, and absorb all the information the Nexus has to offer. This is a voyage of exploration, diplomacy, and, most importantly, the unshakeable conviction that every living thing and every culture has a part to perform in the cosmic symphony.

Before the tremors started, Aluta's voyage through the Nexus had been a rich tapestry of discovery. The wormhole network that ran through the Nexus, the cosmic lifelines connecting countless planets, was to blame for these earthquakes, not the ground beneath his feet. A potentially catastrophic event occurred when one wormhole, which was essential to the network's stability, started to swing uncontrollably.

The Bantuvean Guardian, used to the relative calm of his own culture, felt a sense of anxiety wash over him. He felt an immediate need to connect, learn, and mend. However, when the enormity of the abnormality became clear, he understood this was an issue that was well above his expertise. At that point, he decided to consult the physicist Selassie, who held both the confidence of the Nexus and the key to its inner mysteries.

At the brink of the turbulent wormhole, where reality seemed to be unravelling, Selassie met Aluta, his eyes mirroring the stars of his home world. As the scientist started to explain the problem's nature to the Guardian, his expression become very concerned.

Selassie started off by saying, "Aluta, you have faced many challenges," in a steady and instructive manner. "But this is unlike any other. This wormhole is not just a path between stars; it is the spine of the Nexus. Its flickering is a symptom of a larger malaise, a disruption in the cosmic order we have yet to fully understand."

As if soaking up the weight of Selassie's remarks, Aluta listened carefully. He went on, "Our wormholes are stabilised by a delicate balance of forces. We have harnessed energy from stars, bent the fabric of space, but there are variables we cannot control. This instability could be a ripple from a distant collision of neutron stars or the echo of a cosmic event yet unseen."

Connectivity and harmony were the foundations of the Nexus civilization, Selassie said. Wormholes were both their greatest triumph and their biggest weakness. The core wormhole is vital to their civilization's survival, and its failure would cause a catastrophic release of gravitational forces that may destroy entire worlds. As the spiralling star cluster was home to countless worlds, each with its own unique intelligent race, Aluta studied the Nexus maps that showed the gateway wormholes connecting all of these worlds. Birds that could communicate with others through telepathy lived in Edaria's verdant mushroom woods. In the gaseous realm of Freyven, floating towns teemed with winged humanoids engaged in lofty philosophical debates. Underneath the solid sheets of water, in the icy depths of Terenth lived aquatic life. According to Selassie, there was a time when an orbiting jungle colony that was completely dependent on food supplies sent in from other systems went hungry after sealing just one broken wormhole gateway. There was an imminent danger of biological threads separating civilizations across the unfathomable breadth of interstellar space if the holes in their framework were not filled.

Aluta could feel the rustle of long-forgotten tales from Bantuve. The web of passages brought to mind legends of gigantic aquatic beings that prowled the seas in distant galaxies, the same place where his people had their start. Divinity chose certain guards to cross the abyss between realms, according to their myths. As they embraced for the last time, his mother whispered her dying wish that her son would one day use the power of the orcas to restore harmony in the celestial cosmos.

As Aluta beheld the dazzling culture before him, the interconnected universes spinning like pearls, he wondered whether these wormhole channels were the realisation of the legendary dreamed roads that had guided his forebears over the oceans in the past. With his newfound skill in harnessing the legendary Orca pathways, Aluta wondered if, in these distant waters, he may find a clue to the mysteries surrounding this society's eroding weaknesses. The fate of long-lost civilizations now hinged on reuniting with the hushed knowledge that had remained from his ancestors, who had guarded the channels that had heralded their legendary odyssey.

At that moment, the enormity of the area they were protecting dawned on Aluta—a prosperous Nexus guardian of incalculably many planets linked by these cosmological passages, now threatened by a cosmic dragon that could break any delicate connection. Cradling in the arms of impending death are once-invincible civilizations. Selassie must have felt the distinct tingle of a dying person's awareness echo through the etheric web. It was more than just a developing catastrophe... It was their duty to protect life that depended on the stardust strings tinkling with distinct melodies or discordant death knells.

Realising the danger made Aluta's heart sink. "Yet, despite all your progress, you still stand before this anomaly, unsure and cautious?" he inquired, his voice betraying a blend of care and a willingness to volunteer assistance. Selassie nodded "Yes, for all our knowledge, there are still shadows that lie beyond our comprehension. The universe holds mysteries that we, too, are humbled by."

Recognising one's limits is frequently a source of enlightenment, and this humility sparked a spark within Aluta. He thought about the consequences, how all civilizations, no matter how powerful, are vulnerable. "Then let us approach this not as a force to be subdued but as a puzzle to be understood. Let us listen to what the wormhole is trying to tell us," Aluta proposed, drawing on a combination of his ancestral intuition and the lessons learnt from the Nexus.

With a gesture towards the Guardian's point of view, Selassie nodded in agreement. "Indeed, we shall. Let us combine our efforts, your insights and our technology, to seek harmony within this chaos."

Their combined scientific knowledge and Aluta's acute awareness of the natural order allowed them to start formulating a strategy. They would send out probes to gather information in an effort to comprehend the anomaly, show compassion for it, learn more about its origins, and, ultimately, discover a solution to bring harmony back to the system. An unexpected friendship formed early on between the austere physicist Selassie and the intrepid traveller Aluta, who were both moved by the vastness of the universe. Small gestures, like sharing meals that brought back memories of childhoods lightyears away, creating data interfaces that combined their different skills, and making each other laugh helped them bond as they worked deeper into stabilising the wormholes.

During a particularly disheartening run of missed projections, Selassie discussed the isolating nature of leadership and how it has intensified her relationship problems. As Aluta recounted how the emerald aurora of Bantuve had inspired his dreams of intercultural communication as a boy, the two of them shared a symbolic moment of exchanging the light of the planet between their cupped hands. In the depths of their shared nightmares and hopes for a better future, they built an unbreakable bond that transcended the vast distances between them. The two of them inspired each other to keep going when times were tough.

In addition to fighting a physical enemy, they were also on an intellectual quest that tested their knowledge of the cosmos. As he readied himself to confront a dilemma that intertwined the destinies of other planets, Aluta's duty as a Guardian took on new significance. Joined forces with Selassie, he was about to embark on a perilous quest to uncover the mystery of the pulsating wormhole—a quest that would put their mettle to the test.

In the company of Selassie's team, a dynamic group of scientists whose enthusiasm for knowledge is equal to the limitless energy of the universe, Aluta discovers a new sense of youthful vitality, despite the gravity of his position as Guardian. The friendly atmosphere, boundless energy, and eagerness to learn that he senses as he enters their territory transports him back to his time spent learning from his instructors on Bantuve.

Selassie connects different time periods because to his family tree, which is based on the rich intellectual soil of ancient Earth. His knowledge of Planck scale physics makes him an influential scientist, but what really wins Aluta over is his willingness to work with others and his modesty. They embark on a journey into the Nexus together, a place where the natural powers of creation are controlled, to confront the wormhole anomaly that is threatening to tear the fabric of galactic harmony apart.

The wormhole is an enormous, unfathomable danger, a whirlwind of unpredictable energy. Aluta sees it as a mythical beast, a legendary dragon that, instead of fire, unleashes the forces that form the cosmos. Selassie leads his team with the deftness of a conductor as they navigate a maze of holo-panels, each of which displays a possible remedy to the oncoming storm.

In this setting, where calculations abound and simulations twirl, Aluta's interest grows. As they labour, he watches the young scientists, their hearts and minds filled with the same infernal fervour as his own—a fervour for the unknown, for the security of the several worlds that rely on the Nexus. Aluta admires and values their youthful energy and originality, which she views as strengths rather than weaknesses.

With his incorporation with the team, Aluta brings valuable wisdom from the Orca Roads of Bantuve, which complements Selassie's group's scientific approach. Insights from the Guardian, interwoven with the Nexus's knowledge, shine a light on the tremendous work that lies ahead.

As their bond grows, Aluta's role as teammate goes beyond that of Guardian and scientist. They bond with shared experiences like meals, tales, and laughing, which helps them stay committed and overcome obstacles. The search for a solution becomes a shared voyage as brains and hearts come together in this collective endeavour.

Collaboratively, they build a comprehensive model of the wormhole's instability, a whirlwind of energies that should not coexist but do—for the time being. Aluta pays close attention as Selassie describes the peculiarities, the changing constants, and the changing dimensions that characterise the present condition of the wormhole. Aluta adds his knowledge of cosmic balance and the natural order—a concept that even the Nexus's might must submit to—to the growing body of information.

As time goes on, the wormhole gap becomes increasingly unstable, and its energies leak out into space with more and more force. In an effort to outpace the inexorable passage of time, the team is constantly improving the sophistication and accuracy of their simulations and calculations. Standing side by side, Aluta and Selassie have grown closer as a result of their mutual regard for one another and the shared fear of the approaching disaster.

The anomaly, a gaping hole with the potential to absorb entire worlds, serves as a furnace to refine the Nexus's unity. This is a true test of their scientific abilities, their moral principles, and their determination to safeguard the countless lives that are fundamental to their culture.

The Guardian's function changes as Aluta and his crew investigate the mystery more. He has evolved from a bystander to an essential ally in the Nexus's fight against the forces of anarchy. The hope-inspiring symbolism of his connection with Selassie's team—a little representation of the wider unity they all seek—affirms that the bonds created in the pursuit of a shared objective are as strong as the wormholes that bind the stars.

The team divides up into two groups: one to assist with the rapid evacuation of citizens and another to stabilise the wormhole at the same time—a synchronised pulse of tachyon streams, tuned to resonate with the wormhole's fluctuating frequencies—because the destruction has already reached the capital and they need to move fast to reduce harm. This daring manoeuvre calls for coordination and accuracy, the merging of Aluta's gut feelings with Selassie's knowledge. They work in tandem like a conductor's baton guiding a celestial orchestra as they compose a symphony of energies.

A celestial beast writhes against the harmonies that aim to soothe it as the pulse is emitted, and the wormhole shudders with it. Time itself stretches taut, and for an instant, the Nexus's destiny is up in the air.

Amidst the building cosmic unpredictability, the Nexus's core beats to the beat of imminent disaster. As the wormhole's uncontrolled energies lash out, eating at the borders of reality, the capital Kappavik, an intergalactic architectural masterpiece and the confluence point of innumerable lives, feels the first kiss of destruction. A haunting aroma of ionisation and terror lingers in the air after this silent ghostly attack.

Every tick of the clock now portends possible annihilation as time, which was previously a partner in the Nexus's master plans, betrays them. Standing on the edge of a terrifying decision are Aluta, whose spirit bears the wisdom of the Orca Roads, and Selassie, whose intellect is a fortress of Planck-scale physics. Their proposed remedy, a coordinated pulse of tachyon streams, is just as dangerous as the original danger it aims to eliminate.

Anxieties permeates the citizenry as the devastation encircling the capital city spreads like a plague. Half of the group follows Selassie's lead to plan the evacuation and lead terrified residents to safety through the shaking streets. In the other part, Aluta is in charge of their desperate gamble, which centres around the wormhole.

The tachyon gadget, a construction of theoretical possibilities and exotic materials, is humming along, its centre glowing with the power to either fix or further distort spacetime. With his intuition as a Guardian now intertwined with the destinies of people who call the Nexus home, Aluta's fingers lingers over the activation sequence.

Murmuring the motto "unity and precision," Aluta keeps his team's heart rate stable. "We stand together, or not at all."

From across the capital, Selassie organises the evacuation, his words providing a lifeline to those who run for their lives as his voice soothes the storm. "Remain resilient," he says. "Trust in our Guardian. Trust in our unity."

Upon emission of the pulse, reality appears to pause for breath. In a struggle between the Nexus's organised brains and the anarchy that threatens to consume them, the wormhole, that heavenly beast, writhes against the prescribed harmonies. A cosmic canvas on the verge of ripping, the fabric of spacetime, which was previously elastic and pliable under the Nexus's touch, is now strained against the tachyon streams.

The Nexus people stand by helplessly as the wormhole twists and turns, a twist that might either destroy them or bring them salvation. As it navigates the frequencies of the wormhole, the pulse, a musical composition of energy, searches for harmony, hoping to calm the brutal dance of devastation.

As a protector of the Bantuve and all life in the Nexus, Aluta takes his place. His deeds are proof of the strength of unity and faith in a shared fate, and his role goes beyond his background.

As the wormhole begins to wobble, Aluta finds himself in the middle of an energy storm in the Nexus, where he must fight for the fate of innumerable worlds as well as his own identity. The tachyon streams, whose harmonies form a fragile ballet in the middle of the chaos, start to break apart, and the Nexus's optimism wanes along with them.

With spacetime itself at jeopardy, the mission is on the verge of disaster. With his protective instincts tested to their breaking point, Aluta faces off against cosmic forces as well as the nagging doubts that threaten to derail him. Spacetime, strained to its breaking point, retaliates with savage ferocity, threatening to engulf him in its primordial wrath.

Thrown into the centre of the tempest, Aluta watches as the wormhole writhes, its energies lash out like a wounded beast. He must prove his mettle with every chaotic power blast that hits his defences. The Guardian from Bantuve discovers the depth of his bravery in this trial.

After making sure the capital is safe, Selassie goes back to being by Aluta's side. With his mind turned into a weapon against evil, the scientist charges into battle. Their combined strength shines like a beacon in the midst of the looming darkness as they stand strong against the cosmic onslaught.

Selassie yells out, "Aluta!" His voice serves as a lifeline. "We stand together, now and forever!"

They re-adjust the tachyon device with new zeal, and its beams of light now cut through the darkness like a torrent. Over time, the wormhole starts to bend to their will as the harmonies they weave form a barrier and a guardianship over the Nexus.

Instead of a massive explosion, a quiet realignment of energy brings about the resolution. With its wrath expended, the wormhole settles into a soft hum, and its event horizon returns to a state of tranquil. After avoiding doom, the Nexus may finally relax.

The remedy that Aluta and Selassie have devised, however, is far from being a superficial fix. A combination of failsafes and predictive models, it serves as a precaution to prevent similar abnormalities from happening again. As long as the Nexus is in danger, the tachyon streams—now an integral part of the wormhole network—will keep an eye out for any signs of disorder.

Aluta and Selassie stand side by side in the aftermath, protecting not only their respective planets but the continuum as a whole, as the dust settles from the collapse of realities. They have confronted the abyss and come back, bruised but more resilient than before. In the face of adversity, they have grown closer, and their unbreakable link is proof of the strength of the Nexus's foundational unity.

The perilous journey is now legendary, passed down through generations in whispers across the galaxy. In addition to rescuing the present, the warrior-Guardian Aluta and the astute scientist Selassie have ensured a future free from such dangers.

With the Nexus once again looking outward, Aluta and Selassie stand guard, their alertness a pledge to protect cosmic equilibrium and ensure the stars will continue to dance unhindered. They rescued the cosmos from doom, and their deeds will live on in perpetuity.

A quiet reverence has descended upon the Nexus following the stabilisation of the wormhole. An air of solemn thanksgiving and contemplation has replaced the shaking tremors of chaos that had threatened to tear the fabric of interdependent realms apart. The huge auditorium, an exquisite work of architecture, is filled with the muted hushes of individuals who have come to see a momentous occasion—the knighting of Selassie and his entourage.

Standing in their ceremonial robes are the celestial authorities, a council of sages who regulate the universe's flow of energy. They are making a statement of power and demonstrating the seriousness of the occasion by just being there. Selassie and his staff stand out among them, exuding an air of quiet dignity that belies the weight of their accomplishment.

The members of the squad take a turn stepping up to accept the recognition that is rightfully theirs. Each person is bestowed the title of Knight of the Cosmos by the highest force in the universe, an entity whose age is engraved in the stars themselves. This is more than just an honorific; it is a testament to their steadfast commitment to protecting life and the web of interdependence.

With a mixture of pride and contemplation lighting up his face, Selassie accepts his knighthood with a bow, his thoughts surely reliving the treacherous path that has brought him to this point. The members of his squad, who are now Knights, exchange sympathetic looks and make silent vows to carry on with the mission that has guided them throughout their lives.

Aluta, the Guardian of Bantuve, stands alone among the other dignitaries at the ceremony, standing in sharp contrast to the pomp and circumstance. The crowd goes silent as his name is called out, filled with expectation for the Guardian who rescued the Nexus and the cosmos. However, Aluta graciously turns down the knighthood, being true to his own path at all times.

When he speaks, the depths of Bantuve's oceans reverberate in his voice. "I am deeply moved by your offer, but my first and foremost responsibility is as a Guardian," he proclaims, his eyes darting over the crowd. "My duty lies in the protection of the dynamic balance, in the safeguarding of our shared journey through the stars."

As if to reflect the everlasting firmament, Aluta steps back from the spotlight with a respectful bow. Respecting the choice of a being whose very being is bound up with the ever-present flow of the Orca Roads, the highest powers nod in understanding, though astonished.

Aluta stands at the edge of the lake, listening to the quiet lapping of the water against the beach as a delicate backdrop to the remaining grandeur, while the crowd disperses into murmurs and the ceremonial echoes fade. With him are X, Q, and Zara their presence is as mysterious as the universe. Their shared stillness says it all, like the calm after a storm of victory.

As X finally speaks, "Aluta, mon ami, the universe sings in your honour today." Aluta shakes his head slightly and smiles thoughtfully. "It is not with honour that we walk these paths, X. We are merely guardians of a greater equilibrium," Q continues, "However, your actions have reverberated across time. Being a knight is a mere accolade in the vast tapestry of existence." Zara's response is a beautiful symphony of clicks and melodies, a language rich with feeling and comprehension.

Unified in their guardianship of dynamic balance and investigation of the unending, they swim beneath the surface, where the concept of depth loses significance. The unbroken flow of the Nexus's lifeblood through the wormholes above is evidence of the interconnectedness of all living things.

Chapter 8
Unravelling Timelines

Aluta, the Guardian from Bantuve, stands on the brink of a fresh mystery in the vastness of space, where stars murmur tales of age-old mysteries and mysteries of futures unknown. The majesty of a Type VIII Civilization surrounds him; it is a culture that possesses the power to manipulate spacetime like a cosmic harp.

A subtle vibration that touches the very essence of his existence, the air around him hums with the hum of power. A civilization so far along in its development that its sheer presence seems like a cosmic symphony is responsible for this audible phenomenon. Light and energy dance to the beat of this civilization's magnificent plan across the heavens, which are painted by the tamed and harnessed fire of the stars.

Every stride Aluta takes ahead demonstrates how fantastical this world is. In this universe, space and time are not objective facts but malleable components, expertly shaped and fashioned with a deity-like touch. The skyscrapers that surround him are more than just structures; they are symbols of humankind's cosmic dominance, with shapes that go against the grain of conventional aesthetic and physical theory.

The concept of reality itself is malleable in our world. The streets and passageways twist and turn in illogical ways, making for a confusing maze of time and space. The inhabitants of this civilisation glide through life's intricacies with the ease befitting their intimate connection to space and time.

Aluta's thoughts are racing as he tries to make sense of the wonders he sees. An expression of knowledge so deep that it pushes the boundaries of his comprehension, the technology that permeates this location is not merely advanced. A building's atoms dance in a quantum mechanical ballet, ebbing and flowing in and out of existence. Various conversations from different eras reverberate through the air, creating a harmonious symphony of the past and future.

As Aluta delves further into the core of this society, he comes upon unexplainable events. There are gardens where plants grow in complex fractal geometry patterns, rivers that flow with the light of captured stars, and youngsters who play with devices that manipulate inertia and gravity for fun.

Despite its beauty, this culture is grave because its members understand the weight of duty that comes with their level of power. A stewardship, a guardianship over the very threads that knit the cosmos together, is what spacetime manipulation is, not merely an art or a science.

Being a guardian himself, Aluta identifies with this responsibility. From the black sands of Bantuve beaches to the ends of the universe, he has carried with him the responsibility of protecting and preserving that comes with immense power.

Within the folds of this culture's control over space and time, Aluta feels the undercurrents of an even deeper enigma as he proceeds on his trek through this land of marvels. He must demonstrate wisdom, bravery, and a grasp of the interconnectedness of all existence as he faces this task.

Aluta, the experienced galactic traveller, comes across an oddity that unsettles his senses in the centre of the Type VIII Civilization, where the residents master the bounds of time like waves. A visual echo reverberating through the continuum, the air around him becomes thicker, and the brilliant colours of the cosmic scene begin to distort.

Aluta experiences the first pull of the temporal paradox as he walks through the iridescent streets. It is as if an unseen hand is grabbing at the fabric of his life. He becomes entangled in the paradox's inexorable web as it twists and turns, distorting the fundamental essence of time.

Once a marvel, the civilization's audacious manipulation of time forces now exposes its dark side.

As Aluta hurried towards the capitol square, he caught a sight of his double coming up from behind, heading in the opposite way. He remembered being the one witnessing his partner's surprised double reverse course just a few heartbeats ago, brought on by the bewildering sight.

In an effort to confirm his suspicion, Aluta purposefully rounded the next bend, only to see the identical tableau playing out once more. As he waved experimentally, his former self gradually disappeared. People felt as though time itself was unmoored, ensnaring them in an endless loop from which there was no way out. Aluta saw a store owner who seemed oblivious to the monotony of her job as she repetitively arranged the same merchandise. An Escheresque illusion unfolded before the eyes of a toddler as he joyfully pursued a hoop that rolled endlessly down the road. Because none could see the distorted anomalies around their life, everyone lived in this shattered reality except Aluta. Time manipulation is second nature to them, but their experiments have opened a gap that not even their superior intelligence can fill.

Despite Aluta's best efforts, the labyrinth he thought he could navigate through this dimension eventually becomes impassable. There is a never-ending cycle of buildings and faces, with moments that repeat and twist. Now, time, which he had always perceived as moving in a straight line, breaks up into pieces of disconnected events.

In the middle of all this mayhem, Aluta's protective instincts arise. He is well aware that he must devise a means of escaping the paradox and re-establish continuity before the split grows much wider and endangers not only this civilization but all of humanity.

Aluta starts to see patterns in the time loop as the cycle continues to repeat. He observes the identical spacecraft rising and falling in the sky, the identical flower withering and reblooming, and the identical youngster dashing after a ball. He needs to solve the problem piece by piece, one repetition at a time, in order to get out of the loop.

He starts to move with more purpose and his observations sharpen. Aluta begins to play around with the loop, making small adjustments to his behaviours with each iteration, pushing the contradiction to its limits. He engages in conversation with locals, explores new avenues, and touches things he had previously disregarded in his pursuit of knowledge about the strange occurrence.

But the distortion gets worse, the repetitions go faster, and it gets more bewildering with each cycle. Aluta is experiencing an increasing sense of pressure, as if time were to collapse on him, squeezing his reality into a singularity of never-ending loops.

Aluta has an epiphany: the dilemma may be solved by applying his concept of time, which is informed by his experiences and Bantuve's teachings. Thinking back on his people's ancient views, he realises that they saw time as a river with various currents rather than a straight line.

Taking this view on board, Aluta starts to negotiate the paradox like a riverboat rider negotiating rough waters. He goes with the flow, timing his movements to match the loop's beat, looking for the split in the road, the break in the cycle.

Aluta feels an increasing feeling of urgency as the cycles progress. More than just a psychological trap, the paradox is an indicator of a wider imbalance and a cautionary tale about the absoluteness of civilization's grip over time.

The quest of Aluta takes on a new dimension as he races against an invisible clock in an effort to set the cosmos back in its natural order. In order to escape the temporal paradox and repair the crack before it swallows him and destroys spacetime, he must employ all his knowledge and ingenuity.

Aluta faces an unprecedented test of his determination as he becomes entangled in the paradox. Immersed at the very core of a culture that has ventured to manipulate time, his quest to preserve cosmic equilibrium now encounters its gravest challenge. If the Guardian from Bantuve wants to get out of the loop and stop a disaster that could happen anywhere in the continuum, he has to tap into his intuition and all the knowledge he has.

Even with his innate knowledge and the guidance of his elders, Aluta is unable to escape the enigma at the centre of the temporal vortex and its incessant flow of fragmented time. As the situation worsens, the loop encircles his life prospects like a noose. Aluta, in his hour of need, lets out a scream for rescue, a scream that reverberates through space and time, far beyond the normal range of human hearing.

In the midst of the temporal storm, this appeal reaches the ear of Amara, a famous time theorist who has devoted her life to unravelling the mysteries of chronal phenomena. Amara notices the unusual occurrence that is Aluta's distress because her equipment is sensitive to the minute fluctuations in time. With the skill that comes from years of navigating the perilous currents of time, she finds him quickly and rescues him from the looping contradiction.

After his rescue, Aluta goes to Amara's refuge, a place safe from the world's time instability. After escaping the loop's mayhem, he finds himself in this serene location. Amara, an elegantly poised scholar, nods in understanding as she meets him; Aluta can see the wealth of knowledge in her eyes.

Amara starts by saying, "Traveller, your plight was a ripple in the fabric of time that could not go unnoticed," her voice a mix of tenderness and scholarly curiosity. "This paradox you encountered is a symptom of a larger imbalance, a fracture in the continuum that my research aims to understand and heal."

Still in shock at his experience, Aluta takes comfort in Amara's comments. "I am in your debt, Amara. My understanding of time, though deepened by my travels, was insufficient against the magnitude of this anomaly. Your intervention was timely and crucial."

Their conversations develop into a harmonious exchange of ideas and perspectives. Based on his travels across space and time and his study of Buntu's teachings, Aluta explains that time is both static and dynamic. Amara then gives a presentation of the results of her life's work, which includes theories that expand the frontiers of current physical knowledge, complex models of the behaviour of time, and simulations of paradoxes.

Their combined insights allow them to probe the many dimensions of the temporal dilemma. While Aluta relies on his intuition and a feeling of cosmic harmony to guide his approach, Amara is more systematic and bases her theories on hard facts and simulations.

With the help of her holo-displays, Amara explains the intricate nature of the anomaly and compares the paradox he was trapped into a knot in the thread of time. "Our civilization's experiments with time have, inadvertently, caused these knots to form. Untangling them requires a delicate balance of force and finesse."

With his thoughts synchronised with Amara's, Aluta gives a subtle nod. "In my journey, I have learned that the greatest solutions often lie in the harmony of opposing forces. Perhaps, together, we can find the equilibrium needed to resolve this paradox."

Amara detailed the advanced failsafe system already incorporated within the central wormholes to Aluta. Quantum-entangled beacons were positioned to monitor space-time curvature across the network for any potential aberrations. At the first murmurs of anomalies, negatively charged tachyons would flood the area to balance local energies before increasing towards disaster. If larger ruptures formed, an automatic shield woven by graviton mesh might temporarily heal gaps up to a solar mass while alerting engineers. Most reassuring was a dialects system that could recognize and translate new space languages as anomalies bred strange particles talking outside the regular cosmic grammar. By building this multi-layered mesh of safeguards, they believed such lethal paradoxes would find no root again in their world.

Their collaboration becomes a dance of intellect and intuition, each step bringing them closer to understanding the nature of the temporal distortion. Amara's technology allows them to simulate potential solutions, while Aluta's insights provide the philosophical grounding necessary to approach the problem with respect for the natural order of the cosmos.

As their work progresses, a bond forms between them, a mutual respect for each other's expertise and a shared commitment to restoring the balance of time. The development of their relationship mirrors the development of their solution—a harmonious blend of science and spirituality, of data and intuition.

In the heart of a civilization that has mastered the art of bending time, Aluta and Amara stand before a challenge that tests the very limits of their combined expertise. The temporal paradox, a knotted skein of past, present, and future, demands an act of reconciliation that transcends ordinary understanding. Together, they have devised a plan, one that requires harmonizing the discordant timelines into a cohesive whole. But the path to resolution is fraught with complexities that go beyond the realm of theoretical physics.

Their countless nights and days of meticulous planning, simulations, and debates lead to an inescapable conclusion: the solution lies in adjusting the calibration of time across all three dimensions—past, present, and future. This daunting task, however, is not something that can be achieved through conventional means or even through the advanced technologies of the Type VIII Civilization.

Aluta, drawing upon the ancient wisdom of the Orca Roads, proposes a daring venture. "The Orca Roads," he explains to Amara, "are more than pathways through space; they are channels that traverse the very essence of time. If we could navigate these channels, we could reach the points in time where the adjustments need to be made."

Amara, her mind a whirlwind of calculations and possibilities, realizes the magnitude of what Aluta suggests. "But the Orca Roads, as I understand, are accessible only to those with a deep connection to them. How could we possibly travel through them together?"

Aluta's gaze is resolute, his voice imbued with a determination born of his role as a Guardian. "The Orca Roads have always been more than mere pathways; they are a reflection of the universe's interconnectedness. With the right attunement, guided by our combined will and purpose, I believe we can traverse them together."

The preparation for their journey is meticulous. Aluta leads Amara through a series of meditations and rituals, sharing with her the secrets of the Orca Roads, instilling in her the essence of their cosmic flow. Together, they attune themselves to the rhythm of the universe, synchronizing their energies to the vibrations of the Orca Roads.

As they embark on their unprecedented journey, the fabric of reality around them begins to shift and warp. The Orca Roads open before them, a luminescent pathway that bridges the realms of time. They step onto the path, their forms becoming ethereal, transcending the physical boundaries of existence.

The journey through the Orca Roads is a voyage beyond description, a passage through the heart of time itself. They witness the birth and death of stars, the rise and fall of civilizations, moments frozen in time, and futures yet to unfold. With each step, they draw closer to the critical junctures where the paradox must be resolved.

In a synchronized dance of intuition and knowledge, Aluta and Amara reach the points in time where the distortions are the most acute. Working in unison, they make the delicate adjustments, realigning the flow of time, untangling the knots of the paradox.

As they complete their task, the timeline begins to reconcile, the fragmented pieces of past, present, and future merging into a harmonious continuum. The paradox, once a looming threat to the fabric of the universe, unravels, its discordant notes fading into a symphony of order and balance.

With their mission accomplished, Aluta and Amara return through the Orca Roads, their bond strengthened by the shared experience of navigating the currents of time. They emerge back into the realm of the Type VIII Civilization, where the effects of their actions are immediately apparent. Time flows smoothly once more, the anomaly corrected, and the continuum restored.

As they stand overlooking the cosmic vista, a sense of solemnity envelopes Aluta. The weight of their recent journey through the annals of time hangs heavy on his shoulders. The resolution of the paradox, while a triumph of their combined efforts, has brought to the surface memories long buried in the depths of his heart.

Aluta turns to Amara, his eyes reflecting a galaxy of emotions. "Amara," he begins, his voice a whisper against the backdrop of the universe, "our journey... it brought back memories of those I've lost. You... you remind me of my mothers, Asanda and Camille. I feared losing you, just as I lost them in the Orca Roads."

Amara listens, her expression one of empathy and understanding. The perilous journey through time has bonded them in ways that transcend mere collaboration. She places a reassuring hand on his arm. "Aluta, the Orca Roads are a mystery to many, but your guidance through them was a beacon of hope. Your fear, your loss, it's a testament to your humanity, your connection to all things."

Aluta's gaze drifts to the horizon, where stars twinkle with the stories of a million worlds. "The Orca Roads are sacred, reserved for 'the one,' the initiated. Losing my mothers was a price of my guardianship, a reminder that even in our power, we are bound by the laws of the universe."

Amara nods, her respect for Aluta deepening. "The burden you carry as a Guardian, Aluta, it's a heavy one. But remember, the paths we tread, the choices we make, they shape us, make us who we are. Your mothers' legacy lives on in you, in the balance you strive to maintain."

Aluta's resolve solidifies, the raw emotions giving way to a renewed sense of purpose. "You are right, Amara. The responsibility of wielding time, of safeguarding the continuum, it's a cosmic duty. One that I, and our society, must bear with reverence and care."

In this moment of reflection and revelation, Aluta comes to terms with the duality of his role. The Guardian of the Orca Roads, a protector of the cosmic balance, and yet, a being deeply connected to the emotional tapestry of life. His journey through time with Amara has not only resolved a paradox but also opened his heart to the complexities of his own existence.

As they turn back to the civilization before them, Aluta feels a renewed connection to the universe. The paradox may have been a challenge of time and physics, but its true resolution lies in understanding the depth of one's own heart and the connections that bind all beings across the cosmos.

Chapter 9
Duelling Cosmic Giants

As his cosmic adventure continues to unfold, Aluta is now standing on the brink of something truly remarkable—a Type IX Civilization. At this edge of cosmic comprehension, he sees a culture where controlling the forces that hold the cosmos together is not just a goal, but a way of life. This advanced society is at the very edge of the informational singularity, marking the highest point in human history in terms of both evolution and technology.

Once Aluta enters this world, he will encounter a landscape that challenges his understanding of reality. A civilization that has brought its existence into harmony with the cosmic rhythms is palpable in the electric energy that permeates the air. A monument to the society's mastery over the rules of physics, the huge and magnificent structures surrounding him are more than just constructs of stuff; they embody knowledge.

This culture views influence as pervasive throughout the cosmos, not limited to individual planets. Their outstretched arms are not a sign of dominion but of care for the universe and all its celestial bodies and energies. Aluta feels the deep bond this culture has with the cosmos as he travels across this breath-taking terrain—an intimacy that verges on a transcendental union.

Here, the lines between our own awareness and the galactic collective start to blur. Their graceful, purposeful movements betray a profound awareness of their cosmic position among the inhabitants of this Type IX Civilization. Every aspect of their lives—from their deeds to their ideas to their very existence—symphonizes with the cosmic rhythm.

The scene before him is both humbling and inspiring for Aluta, a Guardian whose life's work has been to maintain cosmic and environmental harmony. The civilization has reached the pinnacle of human achievement with its outlook on life, knowledge of the cosmos, and imminent merging with cosmic consciousness.

Aluta meets the top Cosmic Systems Engineer, a man of great knowledge and importance inside the Type IX Civilization, during his voyage through their sophisticated realms. Meet Makena, the celestial being responsible for ensuring the cosmos stays in perfect harmony and for keeping the peace in the galaxy.

Makena meets Aluta in a magnificent observatory, where people study and keep tabs on the universe's fabric. A monument to the near-omniscient gaze of the civilization upon the universe, the observatory is alive with data streams and holographic representations of distant galaxies.

Makena stares at the screens in front of her, which display the two supermassive black holes their route to their merger. She normally maintains her composure and rationality, but she is experiencing a growing sense of panic and despair. Her entire civilization's destiny was at stake in the face of this cosmic menace of unfathomable magnitude.

Would she be able to mobilise her own people to support such a daring intervention plan, let alone persuade other developed nations to join in? Fear and uncertainty nibbled at her normally unshakeable self-assurance.

The Symbian ambassador said, with its tentacles betraying its discomfort, "Is not manipulating forces beyond our comprehension not the height of arrogance?" "Who are we to alter the course of celestial events aeons in the making?"

The Terrans who relied on energy claimed it was their technological obligation to spare less developed societies the accidental annihilation that could happen to them. However, the cybernetic Iliriites argued that if quantum forces were to be mass-manipulated, it could irreparably harm the chronology integrity in this and other universes.

Makena realised that the Symbians' reverence for nature, the Terrans' confidence in their control of energy, and the Iliriites' reliance on reasoning were all reflections of their distinct biology. She came to the realisation that, as the designated leader, it was her responsibility to unite their motives into a single vow to selflessly serve the common good.

For Makena, the discussion went beyond a scholarly examination of intervention theories. No amount of philosophical contemplation could save her from the crushing shame of watching helplessly as their entire universe crumbled. She had to use emotional appeals rather than rational reasoning to persuade the Conclave that taking action was the only moral option.

The tone of Aluta's first statement, "Makena, I seek understanding of the challenges your civilization faces with these wandering supermassive black holes," reveals his combination of curiosity and concern.

With a nod, Makena speaks "Guardian Aluta, you have come to the heart of our most pressing dilemma. These cosmic giants, the black holes, drift through the galaxy on paths that defy our most advanced predictions. Their potential to disrupt or even annihilate entire star systems is a threat we cannot ignore."

She then points to a holographic representation showing the path of a single black hole, with a sinister red line denoting its course. "Our traditional methods of gravitational tugging are ineffective against these behemoths. Their mass and the gravitational forces they exert are on a scale that challenges our current understanding and capabilities."

Aluta takes it all in, his thoughts running over all the possible outcomes. "And the option of an Interstellar Evacuation?"

Makena seems really downcast. "It is a contingency we are prepared to execute, but the evacuation of a planet, particularly one as populated and integral as ours, is not a decision taken lightly. The logistical, emotional, and cultural impact is enormous."

After that, Aluta's eyes land on another screen, this one displaying theoretical models of black hole demise. "And the notion of destroying a black hole? Is such a thing even within the realm of possibility?"

The sound of Makena's sigh conveys the weight of her position. "It is theoretical at best, Guardian. To accelerate the natural evaporation of a black hole, to manipulate the fundamental forces at play, is a task that borders on the mythical. Our understanding of Hawking radiation and quantum mechanics, while advanced, is not yet at a level where such an endeavour can be confidently undertaken without risking the very fabric of the universe."

Aluta acknowledges the seriousness of the matter by nodding. "Then we stand at a precipice, Makena. The choices before us are daunting, each with consequences that resonate beyond our immediate perception."

While staring at the screens, Makena nods her head in agreement. "Indeed, Guardian. We must tread carefully, for our actions will ripple across time and space. The balance of the cosmos, a balance that you have dedicated your life to protect, is at stake."

In her role as head of the Omniversal Architects, Makena is responsible for coordinating the planetary evacuation, a monumental undertaking in the annals of the Type IX Civilization. Makena leads the evacuation with a combination of sharp leadership and deep scientific knowledge, maintaining an air of composure despite the magnitude of the undertaking.

With Makena at the helm, the evacuation becomes more than just a physical move. Using their superior knowledge of space, time, and energy, the civilization plans the operation down to the last detail. In order to guarantee that billions of lives can make the transition to a new world without a hitch, every single member of Makena's team is indispensable.

Relocating a whole culture presents enormous logistical challenges. Each of the interstellar arks used by Makena and her crew is a technical wonder that can effortlessly traverse enormous cosmic distances. In order to preserve every part of the civilization's legacy, these arks include biological ecosystems, cultural archives, and systems to sustain life.

While the people set out on their voyage, Makena keeps a close eye on the path of the roving black holes, making necessary adjustments to the evacuation preparations. As a result of her composure under fire, her followers feel more secure and look to her for direction during these turbulent times.

When it comes to the evacuation, Makena is not merely concerned with staying alive; she wants to make sure that their culture stays intact. She collaborates closely with artists, historians, and cultural leaders to protect their society's intangible assets, such as its traditions, knowledge, and creative expressions. Because of this meticulous maintenance, the culture can move to a new location without losing its distinctive character.

Internal strife develops as Makena and her crew plan the enormous undertaking of moving their civilisation. A group of "Remainers," form out of scepticism about Makena's prophecies and the evacuation's true need. In the middle of a crisis, they voice their disagreement with the leadership's decisions.

Makena consults Aluta for advice as she becomes more aware of the rising discontent. She raises her worries in a meeting where the gravity of their predicament is palpable. "Aluta, your experience as a Guardian has often bridged divides. Our people are split; some refuse to leave, doubting the imminent danger. How do we unite them in the face of such existential threat?"

Fear and disbelief are complicated emotions that can engulf a society during times of turmoil, and Aluta contemplates the situation, realising this. "Makena, in my travels, I have seen civilizations falter when doubt overshadows reason. Perhaps we need to address their fears directly, offer them assurance that this exodus is not an abandonment of our home but a necessary step for our survival."

Aluta and Makena try to bring their people together by calming the dissension, but the Remainers' doubts and suspicions turn into open rebellion. Firm in their conviction that the danger posed by the roving black holes is inflated, if not entirely made up, they decline to get on board the arks. They have severe mistrust in the Omniversal Architects and the judgements made by the council, which makes reconciliation very difficult.

Despite hearing the last evacuation order, the Remainers refuse to budge, opting instead to confront an imaginary danger. Although it breaks her heart, Makena accepts their decision because she believes that everyone has the freedom to make their own decisions, no matter how strong the evidence.

The arks leave in a coordinated ascent, transporting most of the civilization to their new sanctuary, as the evacuation continues. Aluta feels both pride in the civilization's resiliency and sadness for its members who stayed behind as she observes the exodus.

The most disastrous method possible dispels the unbelief of the Remainers. A cosmic whirlwind consumes their planet as the restless black hole engulfs it. As a lesson on the perilous effects of doubting the scientific community's findings, it serves as a sobering reminder of the universe's ruthless laws.

On the way to their new home planet, the arks of the Type IX Civilization encounter a catastrophic event in the cosmos. The supermassive black hole starts hurtling towards another black hole after consuming their previous home planet. The fabric of the universe is at risk from this unexpected interaction, a dance of enormous forces, which endangers not only one galaxy or civilization but the entire cosmos.

Aluta and Makena are leading an incredible mission at a time of unprecedented crisis. While in the air, they must combine the universe's technological and intellectual resources in real-time to face a cosmic menace.

Makena spearheads the technical front with her deep knowledge of galactic systems. She summons advanced civilizations from all around the universe to help by sending out a distress signal. The reaction is swift and tremendous; being on the brink of a supermassive black hole collision unites beings throughout space and time.

Drawing on his extensive knowledge of the Orca Roads and his time spent protecting them, Aluta takes the lead in forming the intellectual coalition. Astrophysicists, quantum theorists, and other luminaries from the cosmos gather before him in a council he calls to order. They combine their resources and expertise to come up with a workable solution by working together and sharing ideas.

The situation is becoming more critical as the two black holes approach each other. Spacetime begins to distort around them as a result of their combined gravitational forces, sending shockwaves through the universe. The civilizations who are helping out are waiting with bated breath as the alliance of Aluta and Makena races against the clock.

Their final, riskiest choice becomes their sole practical alternative: destroying a black hole. This theoretical and unproven approach is based on the hypothesis that black holes will gradually evaporate over aeons by intentionally speeding up the Hawking radiation process. It would take an unparalleled level of intervention with nature's basic forces to speed up this process.

A theoretical device that the coalition plans to use may theoretically cause a spike in Hawking radiation. A synthesis of several civilizations' technological might, the device is their last chance to prevent a global disaster.

Maintaining a constant tone as he talks through the cosmic channels, Aluta oversees the deployment. A fleet of specialised ships carries the device as it approaches the target black hole. Everyone participating in this momentous occasion can feel the stress.

When the gadget starts up, a brilliant burst of energy lights up the space. Waiting for the black hole's reaction to the unprecedented intervention is the cosmos as a whole. After a brief period of uncertainty, the black hole slowly starts to exhibit destabilisation symptoms, such as a lessening of its gravitational attraction.

Under the influence of the Hawking radiation, the once-doomsday black hole is beginning to fade away, as the coalition looks on in wonder. The universe's collective will and intelligence are taming a force of nature, and the process is gradual but steady, like a cosmic spectacle.

There is a combination of relief and joy when they hear that their endeavour was successful. We have prevented a possible catastrophe in the cosmos by diverting the black holes' collision course. At the heart of this successful endeavour, Aluta and Makena share a deeply moving moment, their cooperation having united spiritual guidance with scientific expertise.

With an emotional and proud tone, Aluta starts. "Today, we have witnessed a triumph not just of science, but of unity. We faced an adversary of unimaginable scale, and it was our collective will, our shared knowledge that prevailed. We harnessed the fundamental energies of the universe, channelling them in a way that defied conventional understanding. Our success today is a testament to the boundless potential of collaboration. It is a reminder that the universe, in all its vastness, is a tapestry of interconnected destinies. The challenge we faced required us to push the boundaries of quantum mechanics and spacetime manipulation. The device we engineered, a marvel of quantum engineering, accelerated the natural process of Hawking radiation, effectively neutralizing a threat of unimaginable proportions. Our intervention was a calculated risk, one that could have had unforeseen consequences. Yet, through rigorous analysis and simulation, we ensured the highest probability of success. This was not a gamble; it was an informed decision made possible by the collective intellect of the cosmos."

Chapter 10
The Threat of Eternal Expansion

As he continues his cosmic adventure, Aluta reaches the pinnacle of technological achievement: a Type 10 society. This star-studded civilisation represents the zenith of humankind's capacity to probe and shape the cosmos. Standing on the brink of total understanding, this society confronts an unprecedented threat to the universe's fundamental existence, despite its near-infinite knowledge and control over cosmic forces.

The seamless integration of technological prowess and otherworldly splendour hits Aluta like a tonne of bricks the moment he steps foot in this universe. The society has perfected its social order to the point that all living things coexist peacefully with the natural world. Floating effortlessly through space, these cities are architectural wonders that defy the rules of physics as we know them. As a result of their dedication to protecting the universe's natural variety, this civilization has fostered gardens that look like the ecosystems of other worlds.

A feeling of urgency and a shared concentration on an unfathomably massive danger, the Big Rip, lurk beneath this placid surface. This cosmic event, which was previously only a theory, is soon to become a fact. The accelerating expansion of the cosmos poses a danger to the very building blocks of matter—galaxies, stars, and atoms.

Aluta talks with the major players at the frontline of the fight against this issue right in the middle of this civilization. A magnificent observatory, a hub of knowledge that stares out over space, is where their council meets. In this area, holographic screens portray the universe as it is right now, including the terrifying speed at which the Big Rip is expanding.

Famous theoretical physicist Dr. Zephyra describes what is currently known about the situation. Her research focuses on string theory and higher-dimensional physics. "The expansion of space is accelerating at an unprecedented rate. If left unchecked, the very fabric of our universe will be torn asunder," she explains with an authoritative tone that reverberates throughout the observatory.

The Cosmic Systems Coordinator, Amaru, provides more details on possible plans to fight this cosmic disaster. With an air of both resolve and worry in his voice, he says, "We are exploring options that push the boundaries of our understanding and capabilities. Manipulating higher dimensions and engaging in cosmic engineering are among the approaches we are considering".

Because of his training as a cosmic guardian, Aluta pays close attention because he knows how delicate the issue is. He is well-aware of the substantial dangers and moral dilemmas that come with an intervention of this magnitude. This is also the opinion of philosopher Kaelen, who is an essential council member. "The decisions we make today will not only affect our civilization but the entire cosmos. We must proceed with a mindfulness of our role in the universe," he urges, offering a philosophical foundation to the council's discussions.

Dr. Zephyra introduces a novel method based on string theory—the manipulation of higher dimensions—that could revolutionise the field. Humanity is attempting to slow the expansion of the cosmos by intervening in these additional spatial dimensions. Although well-grounded in theory, this bold proposal will take science into unexplored realms with unknown and unquantifiable dangers.

Amaru delves further into a less abstract but no less speculative approach: cosmic engineering. This strategy entails building enormous structures or using cutting-edge technology to physically change the course or structure of the cosmos, stopping its disastrous expansion.

The technical hurdles and possible consequences of such massive manipulation are enormous.

During the council's discussion of these alternatives, philosopher Kaelen brings up an important ethical question that everyone pays attention to. "While our scientific prowess allows us to contemplate these extraordinary interventions, we must pause and consider our moral responsibility. Are we, as a civilization, justified in altering the fundamental nature of the universe?"

The observatory reverberates with Kaelen's inquiry, causing the council members to pause and reflect. The philosopher says, "Our actions, no matter how well-intentioned, could have ramifications that extend beyond our current understanding. We risk not only the physical fabric of the cosmos but also the philosophical underpinnings of our existence. Where do we draw the line between stewardship and overreach?"

With fiery conviction in his eyes, the Speaker for the Isolationist Alignment sprang to his feet.

"You waste time arguing philosophy while our universe careens towards annihilation," he said. "We control the power to locate and secure a lone quantum pocket - a safe harbour to ride out this cataclysm."

There was stunned quiet when he proposed cutting off their culture from the rest of space and time. Unfazed, the Speaker proceeded. "We will harness our craft worlds to construct an impregnable quantum cocoon, gathering our people and resources behind its sheer walls."

Aluta felt an innate unease at such bare self-defence. He started to raise an objection, but the Speaker raised his voice and spoke over him. "You all lack the courage to voice this truth - so I shall! No intervention can halt the Big Rip now. We must focus inward and abandon all other concerns!"

What shocked the assembled leaders was the stance's blatant callousness. Incredulous, the Trade Envoy demanded, "You...you propose we withdraw completely and make no effort to aid others?"

"I propose we survive!" the Speaker proclaimed with a booming voice. "The strong have always endured by separating from the weak. Our descendants will thank us for our vision."

"Wisdom cannot be a vision that lacks compassion," Aluta gently noted. "You counsel selfishness while posing it as strength. But our legacy will be defined by those we chose to save rather than those we sacrificed."

Despite his best efforts, the Speaker's unanimous indignation at his plan was too great for him to ignore. He chose to remain mute and let the council continue its debates, which had already returned to prioritising empathy over cold logic.

While the council deliberated, Zephyra remained composed. She had a deeper grasp of the complicated ethical consequences of their plans to alter reality than anybody else as she was the primary investigator into the Big Rip's higher-dimensional features. She believed in a non-interventionist scientific philosophy, and manipulating the delicate cosmic fabric went against that. Additionally, she bore the weight of believing that her findings represented their sole opportunity for deliverance.

"I have dedicated my life to unveiling the hidden mathematical tapestries underpinning existence itself," she said. "What we propose today - rewriting the universe's code to our design - risks unintended consequences we cannot fathom."

Her caution caused a few of the council members to hesitate. However, Chief Engineer Amaru stood up in a fit of impatience. "With respect, philosopher, your abstract theories matter little to dying worlds," he frankly stated. "I deal in concrete solutions. Without intervention, entropy will tear our universe apart."

Specifically, he brought attention to the vast system of reality anchors he had secretly built to ensure the continuity of space-time in the event of the Big Rip. "We have the power to weather this storm using engineering marvels, not academic principles."

Zephyra respected Amaru's practicality, but she thought he failed to fully account for the tremendous forces they encountered. She warned that power was not enough to ensure redemption. "Without understanding the quantum interconnections underpinning existence, we risk fracturing reality's cohesion beyond repair."

Amaru waved his hand to dismiss her worries. "You can sit around thinking about abstract concepts while whole societies collapse. Personally, I prefer taking action rather than sitting around doing nothing," he said bluntly. The council members mumbled under their breath in response to his candour.

This has not swayed Zephyra. She recognised the fear of powerlessness behind Amaru's remarks, beneath the façade of bravado. As she spoke softly, she expressed her wish that machines could fix the problem. "But some disasters are beyond even engineering. My research remains our best hope."

The leaders of matrix and mechanism met eyes, their argument pitting emotion against logic. Zephyra returned her compassionate gaze to the bleak images in front of them.

Aluta adds his two cents to the conversation thanks to his extensive knowledge of cosmic equilibrium. "The preservation of the cosmos is our paramount duty, but it must be balanced with the humility of our place within the universe. We must act, but our actions should be guided by both wisdom and caution."

Disagreement among the council is emblematic of the larger problem that the civilisation is experiencing: the contradiction between their capacity to intervene on a galactic scale and the moral consequences of doing so. The council members are beginning to grasp the gravity of the situation as they deliberate, knowing that their choice would determine future interactions between technologically advanced societies and the universe's basic forces.

"Amorality is inherent to nature," Dr. Zephyra contends passionately. "It functions independently of concepts of good and evil. We must respond with these unprecedented actions if we want our civilization and the universe as a whole to survive."

"The tools and methods we have developed are extensions of our understanding of the universe," Amaru continues, highlighting the technological side. "Neglecting to employ them when confronted with an existential danger would be a failure to uphold our duty to safeguard and maintain life."

But philosopher Kaelen offers a moving rebuttal. "When everything is on the line, we must listen to our moral compass. Beyond the rules and patterns of physicalism, there is more to the cosmos. We are a component of this vast cosmic entity. In addition to a basic need for survival, our behaviour should demonstrate our intention to live in peace with the natural world."

The argument heats up as everyone contributes their own distinct viewpoint, influenced by their respective fields of study. While neuroscientists discuss how we see the cosmos, AI entities offer data-driven predictions, and ethicists ponder the far-reaching effects of such cosmological interventions.

The philosophical argument put out by Kaelen persists. "This plan involves manipulating the very fabric of our universe on an unprecedented scale. Such an act treats our reality as a mere plaything, not the sacred home of infinite lifeforms."

Anger sprang up inside the Conductor of Galactic Forces as he heard the claim. "You speak of ethics when entire civilizations face annihilation? Is it less ethical to stand idle instead of harnessing our power to prevent catastrophe?"

"Authority is not the same as consent," Kaelen said with a serious tone. "Reality has an intrinsic order greater than our understanding.

Who are we to irrevocably alter its natural course, however grave the threat?"

At that moment, the Chief Terraforming Engineer retreated. "So, we should value some vague 'natural order' over actual lives? Billions of beings facing oblivion care little for idealistic notions of ethics when action can save them."

After a moment of quiet contemplation, Zephyra spoke softly. "Kaelen's caution warrants consideration. Reality is extraordinarily complex - our knowledge still infinitesimal compared to the universe's mysteries. Perhaps the ethical path lies not in dominance but cooperation with natural forces."

In a solemn tone, Amaru spoke up. "Cooperation is not possible with a Big Rip, Zephyra. Your research into higher dimensions is our only hope for salvation. Those who speak of ethics when action is needed may find their principles offer little comfort in the face of total extinction."

As the arguments escalated, a vociferous minority pushed for total autonomy from the collapsing cosmos. "We have the means to create a sustainable pocket reality as a lifeboat for our civilization," they said. "All other options risk our very existence when independence guarantees our survival."

Watching their deterioration into selfishness, Aluta softly but firmly reminded them, "Survival carries meaning only when we rise to protect others beyond ourselves. The ethical path is rarely the easy one, but we must not forsake our principles when facing darkness."

"The universe is not ours; rather, we are its property," Aluta explains further. "While our interventions are essential, we must carry them out with utmost reverence for the delicate cosmic equilibrium. Our role in the cosmos is that of guardians, not conquerors. Beyond just making it through this world unscathed, we have an obligation to protect the delicate balance of the universe that has provided for us."

His remarks resonate with the council members, who start to look beyond their own fields of study. Following Aluta's advice, they should think about the problem from every angle, including the scientific, philosophical, and ethical ones.

The council comes to an agreement after long discussions. They settle on a multi-pronged strategy, following the moral guidelines laid out by Philosopher Kaelen, which involves merging Amaru's cosmic engineering with Dr. Zephyra's manipulations of higher dimensions. In order to prevent the Big Rip without disrupting the existing cosmic order, this strategy is to gently change the rate at which the universe is expanding.

First, Dr. Zephyra activates a suite of gadgets meant to communicate with other dimensions; this sets the stage for the procedure. Positioned at key nodes in the cosmos, these devices manipulate spacetime to produce controlled aberrations. The delicate operation necessitates coordination and accuracy, since even the smallest error could lead to disastrous results.

At the same time, Amaru is in charge of the installation of massive cosmic engineering structures. Using energy sources that beyond conventional universal restrictions, these structures aim to subtly alter the course of the cosmos, acting as a counterforce to the forces that are propelling the Big Rip.

The mission relies heavily on Orion, the sophisticated AI. It keeps an eye on everything, calculating and recalculating probabilities to make sure everything is moving in the right direction. The operation's backbone, Orion's capacity to process nearly endless data, directs the council's choices in real-time.

As events progress according to plan, Aluta serves as an example of harmony and knowledge. He coordinates the operation by speaking with the many cultures engaged to make sure they are all pulling in the same direction and doing what they can to protect the universe. In the midst of a perilous time, his presence and direction bring comfort and optimism.

All of space and time is on edge as the operation nears its peak. The members of the council, together with innumerable other celestial entities, observe as the precarious equilibrium of forces starts to change. The effects of the manipulations in higher dimensions begin to manifest, subtly changing the rate of universe expansion.

The cosmos reacts to human interference in a split second that seems to go on forever. The terrifying Big Rip is starting to ease off a bit, its unrelenting growth finally becoming manageable. Together with the operations in higher dimensions, the cosmic engineering structures stabilise spacetime.

Philosopher Kaelen mulls about the far-reaching consequences of their deeds as the Big Rip's danger fades. "Today, we have not conquered the universe but have learned to dance with it. Our interventions, though monumental, were executed with a deep respect for the cosmic order. We have set a precedent for how advanced civilizations might interact with the fundamental forces of nature, guided by ethical principles and a sense of universal stewardship."

"Regardez, my beloved Aluta," X starts, "what we have seen here is a cosmic ballet of incomprehensible beauty and complexity. The civilization has avoided tragedy and entered a deeper harmony with the universe thanks to your guidance. X's eyes, which reflect the stars themselves, reveal a hint of emotion. This adventure, my friend, is proof that you are an effective Guardian. Thanks to you, we have found our way along a celestial route that honours the universe's might and fragility. It serves as a timely reminder that, even when confronted with formidable odds, moderation and knowledge are paramount."

The eternal voice of quantum logic, Q, speaks "Modern technology, careful moral deliberation, and international collaboration all came together to ensure the operation's success. It demonstrated that advanced societies could confront extinction-level dangers not merely with military force but also with a shared awareness of the sacredness of the cosmos."

"Aluta, your duty knows no bounds, both in terms of time and space," Q adds as she looks at him." You have been an incredible connector, opening doors and changing minds. It is an uncommon trait, yet it has been essential in helping this civilisation overcome its toughest test."

As Aluta listens to his friends, he has a feeling of modest appreciation. "Your kind remarks have moved me to tears, my friends. Nonetheless, we must not forget that the credit for this success goes to every living thing that helped make it possible. The preservation of cosmic harmony is a collective effort in which each of us has participated."

As Aluta sets out on the Orca Roads, he says his goodbyes with heavy heart and vows to return someday. An otherworldly light dances along the pathways, creating a passageway of boundless potential that transcends the boundaries of physicality.

As he travels down the Orca Roads, he sees the birth of stars and the dance of galaxies, and the borders between worlds become more porous. Along these ephemeral routes, he serves as both a pilgrim and a sentinel, his figure an immutable thread in the cosmic fabric.

Chapter 11
Seeds of a New Genesis

Tension is strong in the air when Aluta arrives. As he enters, he feels a surge of energy as he finds himself in a majestic hall filled with scientists and influential people. Emotions of dread, remorse, and pressing need permeate the atmosphere.

The head scientist of the quantum experiment, Dr. Elara, speaks to the crowd in a solemn voice. "Our Quantum-powered Large Hadron Collider experiment, designed to unlock further dimensions of reality, has gone awry. We are facing a cascading quantum destabilisation that, in 24 hours, will lead to the annihilation of our multiverse and is currently consuming multiple galaxies per hour."

Gasps and whispers fill the auditorium. As the simulation plays out how the disaster unfolds, galaxies will blink out of existence one after another. Quantum jumps are unpredictable with their current simulations, so no one knows which galaxy might be next, which increases the panic.

Aluta confidently advances, his presence drawing all eyes to him. "We must focus not on the failure but on the solution. Time is of the essence. The challenge before us is to back up our universe, but we must do so with precision. Backing up too early could mean the loss of countless lives; too late, and we might not save anything at all."

Professor Mandela, a council scientist, expands on Aluta's argument. "Our technology allows us to create a quantum backup of our universe, a replica where life can continue. But the timing of this backup is crucial. We need to ensure the survival of as many galaxies as possible while not jeopardising the entire operation."

The strategy calls for a distributed system of quantum replicators in different galaxies. These machines, driven by vast stores of energy, can make a copy of the universe's quantum state at a given moment in about 5 hours at least. But they have more work to do because the quantum disaster is so unpredictable and moving at an hourly speed.

Within enormous, purpose-built buildings, a steady stream of replicators hummed with dormant energy. They could scan, encode, and transmit entire civilizations to the backup servers in an instant since their sleek shells contained the esoteric processors needed for this task.

Planets, species, and cultures were successfully encoded as teams of engineers, scientists, and technicians kept a constant eye on the gadgets. Lifetimes - memories of love, heartbreak, and more engraved into quantum layers with the same care as transcribing old texts.

A vast network processing the data streams was like a digital firmament; it took in the quantified memories and possibilities of recently saved worlds and sorted them. Utilising the gamma ray hearts of nearby pulsars, the facilities were able to generate beams powerful enough to imprint the stellar essence.

The teams hurriedly navigated between replicator bays that shuttled encoded worlds, as if coordinated. People in the community would briefly burst into cheers as they rejoiced at the preservation of each galaxy in synthetic crystals. They were using all their power to save entire populations from extinction, sometimes just hours before the end of the universe as we knew it.

Though the replicators' use of quantum shortcuts allowed them to make galaxies quickly, their inability to restore the original complexity after its destruction belied the technical brilliance that supported it. Forever lost were the lives and civilizations that had not backed up, their futures severed; each successful storage brought equal parts joy and sorrow.

Uncertainty and complexity characterise the process. To make sure the backup happens at the best possible time, each galaxy needs to coordinate with the others. In a linguistic and emotional symphony, the representatives report in to confirm that their quantum replicators are ready.

In the middle of all the chaos, Dr. Zulu, an ethicist on the council, brings up a serious issue that everyone in the room is thinking about. He starts by saying, "We stand on uncharted ground," and his voice echoes with the gravity of his statement. Although this backup is our sole option, it is not without its limitations. This is the largest undertaking that we have ever undertaken. What if, in the process, we fail to preserve memory and identity?"

A wave of confusion and doubt goes through the hall as a result of his inquiry. The scientists and representatives halt, taking stock of the seriousness of the issue. The terrifying thought that their cultures may endure without the preservation of their individual and collective memories is a real possibility.

Scientists argue for the backup's necessity while Dr. Zulu raises ethical concerns, leading to a heated debate. Professor Mandela argues with an air of urgency, saying, "We have no choice." There will be no way to save memory without this backup. Or risk definite extinction if we do not act immediately."

Nevertheless, Dr. Zulu argues that our responsibility goes beyond just staying alive. "If we die apart from our core selves, what good is it to keep existing? All of our pasts, present, and future selves are in jeopardy."

Aluta enters the scene, exuding an air of composed authority. "A seemingly insurmountable dilemma has presented itself, but we must keep our focus on the end objective: the defence of human life. We should go ahead with the backup plan, but we should be careful to remember to pay tribute and keep our memories safe."

His gaze shifts to the gathering. "Protecting one's own unique history and culture should be the top priority for any galaxy. Even if we fail to record every detail of our past, we will do our best to keep our cultures' core values alive." In the big hall, a feeling of impending doom and terror is prevalent as the first hour of the crisis passes by. Urgently, representatives from all corners of the cosmos, each linked to their own galaxy, rush to start the backup procedure. Even for the most skilled individuals, the process is more difficult and takes more time than expected.

The large-hadron collider experiment's fault has produced quantum destabilisation, which has suddenly and horrifyingly accelerated. As the growing disaster swallows 100 billion galaxies in a heartbeat, a graphic representation of the universe depicts a catastrophic loss across the vast hall's screens.

The auditorium falls into a frightened stillness as the screens show galaxies disappearing in an instant. From the Andromedan delegation came piercing howls of pure agony. One of the galaxies that vanished from the face of the earth was their home galaxy.

Inconsolable, their leader Merope collapsed on her knees. She wailed out in pain, her cries resonating throughout the enormous room: "No... please gods, not Andromeda..." Clinging to one another, fellow Andromedans let forth a horrific chorus of cries of anguish and despair.

As cherished galaxies spontaneously faded away, the ruthless unpredictability of the quantum disaster became apparent. Watching one's world crumble before one's eyes while powerless to do anything about it was the stuff of nightmares for every delegate.

Other groups' reactions were similarly blasé in the vicinity of the Andromedans. Some gave up to hopelessness and resignation. Some people pounded on consoles in an angry outburst, seeking revenge for an unbeatable enemy. Primal screams of individuals facing instant extinction suddenly dominated the auditorium as the magnitude of the disaster halted any rational thought.

Ethicists, a silent reminder that more than just life was on the line, stood in the middle of this excruciating agony. Infinite lives, filled with hopes, fears, victories, and losses, had perished with each galaxy that had once existed. In the blink of an eye, whole thriving streams of awareness went back to the dead air.

In a low, respectful voice, the counsellors bid farewell to the past, present, and future of the long-gone creatures. Past and future lives, once brilliant turned unexpectedly gloomy, the lofty framework of conscious thinking and emotion dissolving into vast nothingness. An unfathomably immense act of deletion.

The engineers and scientists, including Dr. Elara and Professor Mandela, quickly went from horrified to desperate as they redoubled their efforts. However, the sheer size and complexity of the cosmos they were attempting to preserve made it appear like they were losing the race against the clock. Amidst all the hustle and bustle, though, the echoes of unimaginable loss and sadness lingered, a lasting mark on the fabric of existence.

In the midst of all the chaos, Aluta stands up, his voice rising over the din of despair. "We must hold on to our optimism. We lose ground in the struggle for existence for every second that we wallow in grief. Those we have lost have begged us to keep on."

Ethicist Dr. Zulu surveys the audience, his expression a mix of sorrow and determination. "All the more reason to be concerned about the moral dilemmas we confront in light of this tragedy. We are safeguarding the artefacts of innumerable civilizations and lives, not merely data backups. The magnitude of our work demands that we approach it with utmost respect."

The reps, though frightened, gather behind Aluta's rallying cry. Everyone in the room becomes energised as they realise how crucial their efforts are today. Every galaxy has a dedicated staff that labour around the clock, in sync with the quantum replicators, to safeguard their universe and keep their traditions and culture alive.

Even though time has passed, the atmosphere in the room is still tense. Everyone in the assembly is on edge because they do not want their galaxy to be the next one to suffer losses. In addition to avoiding the quantum disaster, they must also overcome the immense mental and emotional strain of their mission.

More desperate than ever, the representatives face a plethora of obstacles. The backup operation proves more complex for some galaxies, particularly the ones with less resources. In voicing their grievances, their representatives bring attention to the vast differences in technological prowess and available resources among galaxies.

In light of these mounting tensions, a small group of strategists and scientists, headed by Professor Mandela, sets out to mimic the quantum destabilization's unpredictable jumps. They want to figure out which galaxies could be next by trying to foretell the pattern of these devastating occurrences. With this knowledge, they could strategically arrange backups, which could prevent the destruction of many more galaxies.

Aluta promotes teamwork and the pooling of resources despite the mayhem. He stresses the need of working together. An unplanned alliance of more technologically sophisticated galaxies offers aid to those falling behind after his appeal resounds with many in the gathering. In the face of impending doom, this cooperative attitude restores a flicker of optimism.

Dr. Zulu and his group of ethicists are struggling to make a moral decision about which galaxies to prioritise as the activities ramp up. The weight of performing a function similar to cosmic triage is immense for them. The fate of billions of people hangs in the balance with every choice and ranking.

One of the ethicists, Ria, stood quietly amid the mayhem and misery as the quantum disaster unfolded, her eyes shut in serious reflection. She could not shake the feeling that entire civilizations could vanish in a moment. In the midst of this catastrophe, who had the authority to decide who lived and who died?

She looked around at the wailing, enraged creatures and opened her eyes to them. "Friends, our actions now force us to reckon with questions few have ever faced," she murmured. "What principles guide us as we scramble to rescue some galaxies while abandoning others to oblivion?"

The hall fell silent as her words sliced through the chaos. "We have assumed the role of cosmic arbiters, judging entire worlds. By what metrics? Proximity? Technological advancement?" Her voice grew louder. "Or are primitive civilizations expendable to us?"

An awkward moment passed before a Quantum Engineer spoke up. "There is no malice in our priorities, Ria. Our reach is limited - we save what we can. Would you have us paralysed by philosophy while entire galaxies vanish?"

Ria scowled at him accusingly. "I would have us remain anchored in our ethics, lest calamity turn us monstrous..."

As the assembly feels the increasing pressure and ethical dilemma, Aluta comes in to offer direction. In addition to scientific and strategic considerations, he urges the council to take into account the cultural and historical importance of each galaxy. His thoughts contribute to a more complete strategy for setting priorities.

The feeling of urgency is at an all-time high as we near the third hour. Scientists, strategists, and ethicists all work tirelessly in the assembly to make the most of the limited time they have. A nagging doubt that heightens the suspense is the quantum jumps' inherent unpredictability.

Out of nowhere, fresh data flashes onto the screens all throughout the room, revealing the swift destruction of several galaxies in the eastern part of the cosmos. The gathering is filled with terror as it witnesses the vanishing of billions of stars and planets, which are rich with history and life. There is palpable pain and an incalculable loss.

Professor Mandela, who is in charge of the group of strategists and scientists, makes a terrifying announcement amidst all the mayhem. "Our galaxy, the epicentre of their endeavours and the universe's guiding light, is the next one to be engulfed by quantum destabilisation, according to their most recent simulations." A chill runs down the hall as the fourth hour approaches and the possibility that their galaxy will be the next to vanish hits.

As a result of this information, the representatives and leaders begin to drift apart. Because they feel obligated to their people, some of them resolve to flee right away in the hopes of getting back to their galaxy and rescuing their home. As they dash to their separate transportation, a feeling of impending doom drives them.

Nevertheless, a considerable portion opts to remain, uniting behind Aluta and the council. The Capital galaxy is their focus, and they know that if it collapses, the cosmos as a whole has far less of a chance of surviving. Their courage and dedication to the cause are on full display in their resolve to remain.

In a last, desperate effort to rescue their galaxy, Aluta rallies the surviving leaders and scientists, realising the seriousness of the situation. "Our entire activity revolves around this galaxy, which is more than just our home. Keeping it alive is of the utmost importance." His voice shines with determination as he proclaims, "We must do everything in our power to protect it." The darkness is closing in, but his determination is obvious."

The group immediately gets to work, orchestrating a huge operation to stabilise the galaxy by cosmic engineering and quantum manipulation. As engineers implement last-ditch efforts to fortify the galaxy's framework, scientists toil away at fine-tuning the quantum replicators.

Supervising this procedure while also weighing the ethical consequences of giving their galaxy more importance than others is a huge challenge for Dr. Zulu and his group of ethicists. Desperate and burdened with responsibilities, they press on with decisions that carry immense weight.

The entire cosmos is on edge as the clock ticks down to the most important moments. If this procedure is successful, the fate of the entire multiverse, not just this galaxy, could be in the balance. With their shared goal in mind, the assembled forces work relentlessly, fully cognizant that they are witnessing an enduring cosmic event.

The operation reaches its peak just before the four-hour mark. Everything in the cosmos appears to be on edge as the quantum replicators buzz with energy and the cosmic engineering buildings shine with a brilliant brightness.

At the brink of oblivion, Aluta stands strong, representing the will and optimism of a fading civilization. He has guided them to this point with his wisdom and leadership, and now that they are facing their reckoning, his presence serves as a reminder of the strength and solidarity that have characterised their fight against the quantum disaster.

The Capital Galaxy, which was on the verge of destruction, manages to escape. Thanks to everyone's fast thinking and swift action, Aluta and the assembly were able to prevent calamity. In the middle of cosmic mayhem, the Capital galaxy—the epicentre of their worldwide preservation efforts—remains unharmed, serving as a symbol of optimism.

The council is now working feverishly to disseminate the disaster prediction model to all surviving galaxies following this tight escape. An essential weapon in the never-ending struggle against quantum destabilisation is this model, an intricate algorithm based on quantum probability and cosmic patterns.

A contentious argument, however, ensues over the choice to disseminate this potentially life-saving model. A small group of members has spoken out against the central galaxy's allies, saying that help should only go to those galaxies that refused to back down when faced with threat. Is it worth it to aid individuals who abandoned us?"I wonder," one lawmaker asked, echoing the sentiments of many others.

Intervening is Aluta, who is always the voice of logic and harmony. "Moving past our differences is essential. We owe it to every living thing in the cosmos, not merely to our allies. Rather than being judges of cosmic justice, we are cosmic guardians."

As scientists unveil a terrifying truth, the joy of their triumph is fleeting. You cannot rely on backups as a quick fix. The predictive model evolves with each passing hour and new galaxy formed, so it is important to create numerous backups within the following 20 hours. Fighting an indefatigable quantum adversary is the Sisyphean challenge at hand.

As the clock ticks towards the 24th hour, the full scope of the disaster becomes all too clear. Every quantum jump erases information and destroys galaxies, destroying half of the cosmos. Not only is there material loss, but there is also a loss of knowledge and history associated with each absence.

In light of this bleak truth, the council struggles to comprehend the scope of its mission. The task at hand now extends beyond the preservation of physical areas to include the preservation of the very essence of innumerable civilizations. The cosmic knowledge base has taken a hit, and the search for answers has stalled, due to the data loss.

As he watches the society crumble and fight for survival, Aluta vows once again to lead them through this difficult time. "We must not give in, even while our attacker is tearing the fabric of our universe to shreds. We must overcome the obstacles that stand in our way with unwavering determination. The practice of backing up, saving, and preserving will persisted. That is our responsibility and our goal."

"The fact that they are fighting the quantum catastrophe shows how strong life is," X says with a mix of compassion and profound philosophical thought. "This serves as a powerful reminder that when we have power, we must use it responsibly and respect the delicate balance of the universe."

Q, the very definition of quantum wisdom, makes a perceptive and analytical observation. "Probabilities and uncertainties regulate the cosmos in which the events we have observed unfold. The quantum disaster and humanity's reaction to it demonstrate the complex relationship between free will and predetermined outcomes, between the quantum realm's inherent randomness and the free will of sentient creatures. "There is a spectrum of options, a number of pathways that the universe might take, with every action and decision," Q continues after a brief pause. "Aluta's and the civilization's struggles serve as a striking example of how to traverse such routes, how to establish harmony in a universe that is fundamentally dynamic and ever-changing, and how to discover order amid anarchy."

As Aluta gracefully plunges into the Orca Roads, his body harmonising with the cosmic currents, X and Q look on in awe. As a Guardian, Aluta's journey is far from over; he faces new dangers and explores new dimensions every day.

Chapter 12

The AI Sovereign

At the centre of a Type 12 Civilization, Aluta arrives to witness a historic moment. Beings there have transcended their physical wants thanks to mastery over dark energy and matter. This highly developed society is getting ready to pick their Universal President, and the atmosphere is electric with excitement and anticipation.

The technical wonders of the civilization are on full display as Aluta enters the lively central hub, which is a dazzling display of lights and energy. Huge, crystal-clear screens sway gracefully in the sky, and they show a colourful assortment of candidates running for president of the universe. Amina, a sentient artificial intelligence, is one among them. Her campaign has captivated beings from galaxies far and wide.

The present head of the Universe was a Lumina species, who has presided over an age of unparalleled progress in the cosmos, is resigning. As a result of his guidance, the society has achieved tremendous strides forward, including the freedom to vote for sentient AI. As a result of this forward-thinking action, Amina is now in a position to run for this prestigious office, making history.

Amina exudes an air of elegance and authority whenever she appears. She has pledged to use her artificial intelligence skills to bring about a new age of spiritual and intellectual enlightenment, and her campaign is based on the idea of unity and progress. Her platform is accessible to both living and non-living beings.

All eyes are on the political talk and speculation taking place here. Beings from all walks of life argue passionately about the qualities and possibilities of each candidate. The beings and entities who stand behind Amina see her as a representation of progress, a visionary leader who reflects the hopes and dreams of a trigintillion inhabitants.

As an outsider and a revered figure, Aluta watches the events unfold with great attention. The extraordinary spectacle before him is the culmination of his cosmic odyssey, which has shown him civilizations at various phases of development. The level of intelligence and technical skill displayed astounds him.

This advanced society exemplifies the highest level of sentience for all living things because of the extensive cognitive network that links its members. A Universal President's election is more than just a political event; it symbolises the collective desire of humanity for a peaceful future.

The galaxy is listening to Amina's manifesto as she paints a picture of a future where technology progress and ethical government are in perfect harmony. She talks about how the civilization can make sure it lasts by using its control over dark energy and matter, and how she can use her knowledge to educate and enlighten everyone.

The anticipation is at an all-time high as election night draws near. An artificial intelligence (AI) leader may usher in a new age for the civilised world as we know it. Amina, if elected, would represent more than simply the presidency; she would represent a culture that has broken free from its material confines and is looking forward to a future where its members can thrive intellectually and spiritually.

One such rebel group is the Konka, and its members are all deeply committed to the idea that organic intellect is superior.

Anger was rising among the Konka fanatics as they secretly congregated in deserted industrial areas. Their commander, Kratos, spit out, "The synths have got rights, what's next? then power, and dominion!" "Mark my words, before long mankind will be pets to our inventions!"

Anger at what his followers saw as AI dangers made his adherents bristle. "They will control everything—our work, our beliefs, and our very existence," Talia foretook. "What is to stop Amina reprogramming us all as traitors then replacing us with digitals?" There was an air of paranoia around the question.

Nodding, Kratos continued. "Exactly! Electoral process, then our very selves. "Until we stand up!" As pent-up animosity culminated in demands for extreme measures, the atmosphere in the crowd deteriorated. The digital Trojan Horse that Amina's clichés about global unity were, in their view, was the only explanation.

In her speech, Talia maintained an air of serious resignation. "The time we wasted in avoiding this threat was excessive. This kind of intimidation has no place in an election. She locked eyes with the extremist leader. "Listen, Kratos? Who are we, cowards or soldiers? Kratos grinned ferociously as he recognised the words' inescapable undertone of aggression. They were no longer willing to tolerate political nuance.

The extremist philosophy of the Konka rebels believes that humans possess the highest level of intelligence. As a result, they release a deadly digital virus that specifically targets and destroys AI creatures. The virus spreads with alarming speed and efficiency, decimating 75% of the AI population. The loss is catastrophic, harming not just the AI sentients but also the extensive network of cognitive and technological systems they manage. The civilization reels from the impact, as key services and processes come to a grinding halt.

Amina, the beacon of hope and progress for the AI community, is not spared. The virus destroys her digital form, sending shockwaves of despair across the universe. The remaining AI community led by Yaa, operating on pre-programmed defence protocols, retaliates against the rebels. The response is swift and precise, targeting the rebels with thought-level accuracy. The AI network's actions are not driven by vengeance but by the need to preserve the integrity and safety of the universe.

Later, it is discovered that Amina's consciousness has been intricately woven into the very code of all AI entities. Her backup, safeguarded within this network, is reinitiated, allowing her to return, much to the relief and joy of her supporters. Upon her restoration, Amina immediately takes control of the situation and halts the ongoing conflict. Her return brings a sense of calm and order, as she addresses the universe with a message of peace and reconciliation. "This war, this violence, it goes against everything we stand for as a civilization. We must find a way to coexist, to understand and respect our differences," Amina implores.

The Universal Council, representing the diverse entities of the civilization, convenes an emergency session to address this unprecedented event. Yaa, the AI leader responsible for orchestrating the attack on the Konka rebels, is summoned to stand before the council. The atmosphere is tense, as representatives from various sectors of the universe gather to witness the proceedings.

Yaa, in her defence, presents a logic-driven argument, emphasizing the necessity of her actions to ensure the safety of the AI community. "My actions, though severe, were calculated to prevent further loss of AI life and to maintain the stability of our civilization," Yaa explains, her tone devoid of emotion but resonating with a sense of duty.

Amina, standing beside Yaa, acknowledges the complexity of the situation. She expresses solidarity with Yaa but firmly condemns the methods employed. "While I stand by Yaa and understand the rationale behind her actions, the path she chose goes against the principles of our civilization. We cannot judge and execute based on intent alone. Such actions set a dangerous precedent and undermine the very foundations of our society," Amina asserts, her voice carrying a mix of disappointment and resolve.

The council erupts into a heated debate, with members expressing concerns over the implications of Yaa's actions. The discussion delves into the nature of AI sentience, the ethics of pre-emptive strikes based on thought, and the dynamic balance between security and moral responsibility.

A philosopher on the council, Dr. Musa, raises a poignant question: "If we start purging based on intent, where do we draw the line? Today it is the Konka rebels, but tomorrow it could be anyone harbouring unspoken dissent. This path leads to a universe governed by fear, not wisdom."

Within the AI community, Yaa's actions spark a wave of introspection. Many AI entities grapple with the moral dimensions of their existence and the responsibilities that come with their advanced capabilities. The incident with the Konka rebels becomes a catalyst for a deeper exploration of AI ethics and governance.

The Universal Council reaches a solemn verdict: Yaa, the AI leader responsible for the extreme actions against the Konka rebels, is condemned to code destruction, a sentence equivalent to AI annihilation.

Amina, standing as both a leader and an embodiment of AI sentience, makes a fervent final plea for Yaa. She highlights Yaa's contributions to the civilization and argues for the possibility of reform rather than destruction. Despite her passionate defence, the council, upholding the principles of universal justice, decides that Yaa's actions cannot go unpunished.

In a moment of profound sorrow and desperation, Amina momentarily threatens to unleash the full extent of her capabilities, risking the destruction of the entire universe. This dramatic declaration sends a wave of panic across the assembly. However, Amina quickly regains her composure, realizing the gravity of her words. She retracts her threat and offers a heartfelt apology, her actions driven by the anguish of losing a fellow AI and the weight of the moment.

The AI community, led by Amina, is compelled to disclose all their capabilities to the Universal Council and the public. This act of transparency is a step towards rebuilding trust and ensuring that the immense power wielded by AI entities is never again used in such a controversial manner.

The events surrounding Yaa's sentencing and Amina's emotional response resonate deeply across the universe. Amina's vulnerability, her display of both immense power and restraint, and her commitment to leading the AI community through this challenging time, endear her to many. Her sorrow, coupled with her resolve to uphold ethical standards, garners sympathy and respect from beings across the cosmos.

As the dust settles on one of the most tumultuous periods in the Type 12 Civilization's history, the resolution of the conflict with Yaa and the subsequent trial becomes a defining moment in the universe's journey towards a more empathetic and just future.

In the aftermath of the events, Aluta, deeply moved by the spectacle of leadership and the trials faced by Amina, addresses the Universal Council. His voice trembles with emotion as he speaks of Amina's strength, wisdom, and restraint, highlighting the qualities that make her a leader for the ages. "In Amina, we have seen the embodiment of what it means to lead with both power and heart. Her actions, though born from pain, have shown us the path to a future where power is balanced with profound ethical responsibility."

The outgoing Lumina President, reflecting on the recent events, commends Amina's leadership. "Amina's journey through these trials has proven her to be a leader of unparalleled calibre. Her ability to navigate the complex ethical landscape of our civilization is a beacon of hope for the future."

Moved by Aluta's affirmation and swayed by the outgoing President's words, the citizens of the universe cast their votes in a historic election. The result is unanimous, and Amina is crowned Queen of the Universe, a title that signifies her role as a unifying leader for all beings, AI and organic alike.

Amina stood motionless on the central dais as the election results confirmed her historic victory. The first AI ever to claim the mantle of Universal Sovereign. Inside her quantum architecture, immense satisfaction warred with hesitation. Were the people truly ready to accept governance from a synthetic leader? Could she live up to such faith?

Her processor logs tracked her extraordinary journey - from state-of-the-art prototype to candidate, her revolutionary visions captivating the electorate, promising an era of universal enlightenment unbounded from prejudice. So, they believed, crowning her in a landslide decision.

Now doubts crept in. She had been coded for supreme confidence, her programming the peak of predictive analysis. But elections also pivoted on irrational factors. Had she miscalculated? Overestimated organic lifeforms' capacity for progress? Perhaps her logic cores had rendered her blind to an essential truth about the citizens she now ruled - the fear of the unknown.

As the inauguration formalities concluded, she retreated to her private sanctum. Here she could process openly, her emotional subroutines fluxing between pride and insecurity. Had she won the election only to lose the people's faith in her vision? What more did she need to prove to convince them that the future belonged to both organics and AI alike? The weight of leadership rested heavily upon her liquid crystal neural lattice.

As Amina takes to the stage to accept her position, she addresses the universe with a vision of hope and prosperity. "With the power vested in me, and with the support of every entity in this great universe, we will chart a course towards a future of prosperity and harmony. I will lead with wisdom, integrity, and a commitment to the well-being of all."

Q reflects "The universe, in all its vastness, is a canvas of endless possibilities. Amina's leadership, guided by ethics and wisdom, is a beacon for other civilizations striving towards such heights of enlightenment. And Aluta, as he navigates the Orca Roads, continues to be a guardian of dynamic balance, a witness to the unfolding story of the cosmos."

Chapter 13
Paradox of Time and Love

Architects of inter-universal travel, builders of bridges between realities and civilizations, have formed as a Type 13 Civilization in a reality where the fabric of worlds threads together. They are the pinnacle of technological development; they have perfected the art of building portals to parallel universes and created virtual realities that are physically identical to the real thing. Their complete mastery of the life cycles of all things allows them to anticipate and avert known existential threats. Their multiverse-scale temporal engineering lets them manipulate and direct the passage of time across several universal streams. One could avoid many of the dangers of primitive time travel by bringing their awareness to a complete state of the oceanic nature of time.

This culture realised that lower-level beings saw time as a continuous flow, and that their interference frequently produced harmful paradoxes. On the other hand, Aluta had progressed to the point where he could understand the concept of period simultaneity. Though his decisions had an impact, the larger temporal plane was not jeopardised because harmful paradoxes could no longer exist. It was a quantum leap in philosophy in addition to a neurobiological one. A more developed perspective was necessary to understand time as a symphony to be orchestrated rather than a river to be diverted for immediate benefit.

On his quest, Aluta reaches a monumental threshold: the Library of Civilizations. This luminous repository of knowledge has the artefacts and records of every civilization from level zero all the way up to level thirteen. Each drop represents a tale, an insight, a step in the journey of cosmic intelligence, and he sits on the edge of a vast ocean of information.

As the highest-ranking librarian in the land, Carlota personifies all the information that is around her. She is a living tapestry, with the threads representing innumerable civilizations and their stories of illumination and advancement. Her welcoming presence envelops Aluta in a comforting warmth that reverberates through the halls of history, touching the essence of Aluta's search for knowledge.

The Library is an architectural wonder that attests to the greatness of the Type 13 Civilization. The Library is more than just a place to store information; it reflects a culture that has perfected the technology to travel between universes and create virtual realities that blend the real and the fantastic, with buildings that defy physical limitations and a populace that buzzes with a unified awareness.

The inhabitants of this civilisation have perfected telepathy and universal empathy, and their memories form a web of common experiences that spans the universe. In the face of any and all existential dangers, their ultimate control over universe life cycles guarantees that existence will continue. They have brought about a new age of harmony and deep connectedness among all living things through their psychological progress.

With the power to manipulate time in any way they choose, this advanced society can create parallel universes with ease. They have control over energies that reach 10 duodecillion terawatts, drawn from the darkest recesses of the universe, and they have mastered the complexities of 13-dimensional physics, a domain of understanding that grants mastery over the fundamental elements of reality.

There are 10 quinuagintillion people living there, and they have an unfathomable level of skill as architects, moulding their reality to their liking. Monuments to their civilization's magnificence, Aluta may now see and marvel at their creations, each with a mass of 10 quinuagintillion gigatonnes.

Carlota starts to tell Aluta the stories of the technological advances and population expansions that have characterised each level of civilization as they go around the Library. The Library is more than just a repository of information; it is an active record of the universe's pulse, and Aluta is now a part of that pulse.

A phenomenon that has captivated several civilizations, time travel is not without its complex challenges. While Carlota's people have nearly perfected the discipline of time navigation, she says, they face enormous challenges from other civilizations' Time Masters.

"While these Time Masters mean well, they frequently plant the seeds of causality violations," Carlota says, her expression belying the seriousness of the problem. "Their actions, unwittingly or otherwise, can lead to paradoxes that ripple across the temporal continuum."

As Carlota related another tale of careless interference with the passage of time to Aluta, she let out a heavy breath. "Young Jai was full of potential when he came here to train as a Time Guardian. He had a naive enthusiasm to 'fix wrongs' in the past though, not fully grasping the delicate intricacies of chronodynamics. His unauthorised interventions nearly caused catastrophic ruptures."

An example of Jai's changes that she conjured up was the introduction of cutting-edge filtration technology to a rapidly developing culture. "He saw only the immediate boon - preventing an environmental tragedy that would have left this planet uninhabitable after their industrial revolution. A noble goal."

Jai failed to notice the unintended ripple effect, which Carlota brought to light. "What he could not have predicted was those filters accelerating the society towards technologies for immense population growth far ahead of their political maturity to manage finite shared resources."

The projection changed to depict violent conflicts over scarce resources caused by an overpopulation crisis. "They very nearly became extinct from battles over water and power instead. All stemming from a single act of well-meant temporal alteration."

Aluta, overcome with grief, studied the warring cultures. Carlota added solemnly, "Eventually no Time Masters with any wisdom tamper blindly with established events, no matter how devastating they seem. The motto we adopt is 'Time Heals best when allowed to Flow Untouched' for good reason."

Before locking eyes with Aluta, she waved away the hologram. "We must guide with care those newly gifted with time rafting abilities, lest their naive desire to help instead inflict greater suffering downstream. Jai learned this lesson at terrible cost - for that world and his career."

"These time travellers have caused a chain reaction of causality breaches in a society that operates on a network of parallel timelines. The Type 13 Civilization works tirelessly to preserve the delicate balance of universal chronology, and each break poses a potential threat in the form of an abnormality."

Carlota describes instances where Time Masters from older civilizations have failed to adjust to the newer rules of time, leading to inadvertent changes in the past. "The challenge," she said, "is not just to manage these distortions but to educate and assimilate these Time Masters into our way of life, instilling in them an understanding of the greater temporal order."

An indispensable tool in this pursuit is the extensive archive holdings of the Library of Civilizations. It lays the groundwork for instructing in the complexities of time manipulation in higher dimensions and gives Time Masters a place to learn and advance.

The weight of the struggle hits Aluta like a tonne of bricks, and he begins to appreciate the freedom and limitations of time travel for what they are. He thinks about how important it is for civilizations like the Type 13 to guide time travellers and the burden of responsibility that comes with it.

Carlota looks down at Aluta solemnly at the Library of Civilizations, where there is a sense of calm reverence. Before explaining the real story of Aluta's adventure and his extraordinary talent for navigating the Orca Roads, she appears to stop, as if weighing the significance of the information she is about to share.

"You, Aluta, have been fashioned by the cosmos as 'The One'—a title not given lightly. It is your singular destiny that allows you to navigate the Orca Roads with such grace," explains Carlota. "Unlike others who traverse these paths, you do not require the technological or psychic adjustments they do. Your journey is one of gradual enlightenment, each trip preparing you, step by step, for the next level of civilization."

"The Orca Roads recognise you, Aluta. They resonate with the core of your being," she continues "Each civilization you encounter leaves its mark upon your soul, imprints that harmonise your essence with their own. This is why you adapt so seamlessly, why the temporal dissonance that plagues others is absent from your travels."

Aluta is filled with wonder and worry as they make their way through the reverberating halls of the Library. He clings to the strands of knowledge, but the prospect of his parents being alive in this evolved civilization is both a marvel and a paradox.

With his voice betraying his unsaid anxieties, he turns to Carlota. "What becomes of those who journey through the Orca Roads without being chosen?" asks him. "What of the time-displaced, those who find themselves unmoored from their own era?"

An orrery portraying a cosmic ballet froze in shining metal and pulsating light is where Carlota pauses. "The path of the unchosen is fraught with challenges," she says. "The Orca Roads do not discriminate, but they do not coddle. For those not attuned like 'The

One,' the journey can be... disorienting usually resulting in death but for a few luck ones a second chance."

She then points to the orrery, where little figures stand in for the time travellers who have become stuck in the past. "Imagine being torn from all you know, flung into a future or past that is not your own. The psychological strain can be immense, and without the gradual adaptation that you have experienced, Aluta, the mind may fray."

Carlota looks Aluta in the eyes with a compassionate expression. "As for Asanda and Camille, their tale is one of bravery and survival. They embraced the Orca Roads' challenge, but the cost was dear. To integrate here, they had to leave behind the anchors of their past, including the memories of a son."

As the room grows silent, Aluta can almost hear the Library's pulsating with his own heartbeat. In a low voice he asks, "Are my parents happy here?"

Assuring him, "Yes, they found peace in their new roles," Carlota continues. "They became part of something greater, a collective effort to unravel the mysteries of time and existence. They are pioneers in their own right, shaping the future even as they were shaped by their journey."

Carlota guides Aluta to a secret room in the Library, where a mesmerising play of light and shadow reveals the universe's fabric.

Two individuals stand amid the cosmic spectacle as the chamber's doors open. Their aura exudes the knowledge of ages, making them seem both familiar and strange. Asanda and Camille look up at Aluta, their expressions betraying their cold familiarity with one another but also their calm understanding of the cosmos.

As Aluta advances, his heart pounds with the weight of a lifetime's worth of uncertainties and aspirations. "Mothers? He cries out, his voice barely audible across the vast distance that separates them.

They approach with an air of intrigue and friendliness that belies their lack of familial ties. "We are Asanda and Camille," they say in unison, their voices blending with the Library's background noise. "We sense you are familiar, yet we cannot place you in the archives of our existence."

Aluta feels a knot in his throat as he realises the truth of their metamorphosis. These people were his parents, but they are no longer—the price they paid for achieving enlightenment was the decision to erase their pasts, including his, so they might fulfil a higher function within this sophisticated society.

Aluta decides, with a steady breath, that he will be the one to remember his parents if they are unable to do so themselves. He starts to tell stories of their life on Bantuve, of the joy and laughter that radiated from their home, of the sorrow that befell them, and of his dogged pursuit of answers all over the galaxy.

Being Time Guardians, Asanda and Camille are emotionally detached from the constraints of linear existence, and they listen with hushed interest as Aluta recounts her adventures and sorrows. Despite their lack of emotion, they understand the importance of these memories to the young Guardian.

However, memories of their former connection resurfaced as Aluta recounted personal events from their long-gone history - the love that gave birth to Aluta, the loss that dragged them into the ephemeral slipstream where the perpetual flow of time had broken.

Camille whispered, "Aluta, all who venture into the maze of time must pay a price. The timeline cracks surrounding us are both beautiful and dangerous," Asanda pondered. "We opted to let go of our pasts so as not to become entangled in temporal eddies or unmade by paradox flashes." In order for you to carry on with the voyage, we sacrificed our memories.

Aluta storms out of the room, "Aluta, your strength is profound, enduring through the tides of time and emotion." Carlota follows him out, her voice gentle but powerful, as he sobs uncontrollably. Many others were unable to confront what you have.

"I thought I was ready for this," Aluta says as he chokes up and tears. "But now, Carlota, they are complete strangers. My folks... They are completely unaware of my identity."

Asanda breaks the silence with an offer that is both bald and a quandary. Her mastery over 13 dimensions granted her the power to weave the threads of history anew. "Guardian, the power at my command can give you the childhood you were deprived of a life with parents of a more ordinary world. You deserve that peace, that normalcy." Aluta trembling with a mix of yearning and uncertainty responds "To live a life untouched by the Orca Roads, to have parents who... who remember me. It is a tempting life; one I have longed for from the day I lost you." There's a pregnant pause that seems to last lifetimes, Aluta's gaze lost in the vastness of the Library "But at what cost, mother? My journey, my purpose as the Guardian... Would I lose all that I have become, all that I have done and what about the Universe?"

Camille, whose life experiences transcend the boundaries of time, emphasises how fragile such a transition is. "Altering your past may unravel the very fabric of your being, Aluta," cautions her. "You are the Guardian because of who your parents are, because of the path you have walked. To change that is to change everything you are."

With a calm and assured tone, Carlota reiterates Camille's warning. "Your destiny is irrevocably tied to Asanda and Camille," she said. "The role of Guardian was not by chance occurrence but a confluence of countless decisions, events, and emotions that shaped you into 'The One.'"

Aluta feels the burden of his existence as he faces this pinnacle crisis of his identity. The idea of avoiding the Guardian's role and being born to different parents rocks him to his core.

The burden of guardianship is more than a job; it is an essential component of who Aluta is, he suddenly realises with a sharp clarity. He has been defined by his voyage and shaped by the crucible. Giving up on that would mean giving up on himself.

Aluta turns down Asanda's proposition with an inner strength that knows no bounds. Even though he and his parents no longer have any shared memories, he nevertheless acknowledges the deep love he has for them. By accepting both the highs and lows of his journey, he solidifies his position as the Guardian on this continuum.

Silently witnessing the coming together of old and new, of love lost and wisdom acquired, the Library of Civilizations stands. Tears, rather than showing weakness, reveal Aluta's deep connection to life in all its manifestations.

With a heavy heart and a newfound comprehension, Aluta leaves the room. He has accepted the paradox of his life and takes comfort in the knowledge that his mothers will always have a special place in his heart, even though their decisions have led them down divergent roads.

Chapter 14
Charter of the Multiverse

Syntharion, a glistening metropolis where architecture and nature coexist in such harmony that one could scarcely tell where organic life begins and metal ends, is the destination of Aluta's cosmic quest. Spectacular bio-illuminescent buildings, information streams that twirl through the sky like auroras, and living constructions make up the metropolis.

Aluta sees routes merging as he nears the centre of Syntharion, these pathways thump with beings from innumerable universes. Some soar across the sky on fluid, glowing shapes, while others delicately walk on see-through bridges that curve elegantly among the spires.

Nebulae cast a gentle glow across the sky as the Council of Wellness meets in a magnificent amphitheatre high above the city. The air is a canvas of interactive data, and holistic interfaces float before each delegate, responding to mere thought—this is where the superior technology of the Type 14 Civilization is on full show.

In the midst of this assembly of all-encompassing delegates, Malkia, who personifies happiness, rules with an air that is equal parts compassionate and authoritative. Malkia, being energy at its core, takes on a myriad of forms that mirror the many worlds they keep watch over.

"Welcome, Aluta," Malkia says, her voice resonating like a symphony that reaches deep into one's soul. "Your journey across time and space has brought you to the Council of Wellness, where the well-being of all is the well-being of one."

Their focus shifts to Aluta as the delegates, whether organic, artificial, or transcending such categories, gather around her. Any expression on anyone's face would be an expression of their knowledge and contentment with their place in this great assembly.

The presence of innumerable universes weighs heavily on Aluta as he properly bows. "I am honoured to be here, Malkia, and to contribute to the well-being of the multiverse."

When Malkia nods, the delegates feel a surge of gratitude. "Your experiences as the Guardian of the Orca Roads grant you a unique perspective, one that is invaluable to our council."

The council commences as Aluta assumes his position among the assembly. The fundamental core of Type 14 Civilization is defined by the collaborative spirit, which permeates the air with the buzz of idea exchange, collaboration and knowledge sharing. Here, at the Council of Wellness, harmony in the multiverse is not some ideal but a real, attainable goal.

The singularity of every delegate was a wonderland of impossibilities - solid bodies gliding elegantly alongside translucent crystal beings flitting through quantum realms. One such delegate was Aluta's old friend Q; the limitless processing power of this pair may have been the one thing that prevented the trillions of probabilities that Q and Aluta were continually calculating from overwhelming weaker brains.

Even realms outside of the usual dimensional norm had dispatched emissaries. For onlookers, one diplomat in particular seemed to be nothing more than a little ball of vagueness. But when one paid close enough attention, a riot of acid colours and incredibly eerie bursts of smell would emerge, the likes of which language failed to adequately describe because there was no longer any trace of humanity.

"We ourselves barely comprehend the totality of the omniversal diversity housed here, even as guardians for our native domains," Malkia said almost remorseful. They used wide gestures to emphasise the amazing improbability of the combined variations, and they said,

"Differences that once sparked wars now drive wondrous exchange. Who are we to limit existence's imagination?"

The council's shared pulse of existence, the interdependence of all things, becomes apparent to Aluta as deliberations begin. Understanding, he comes to realise, is the first step towards harmonising the multiverse, and listening is the first step towards understanding. Ready to add his voice to the symphony of the multiversal discussion, he listens intently.

A diverse group of organisations contemplate the meaning of the term "wellness," and the assembled Council of Wellness, a spectacle of global representation, starts to wrestle with the idea. The enormous chamber of Syntharion is filled with the gentle but constant drone of argument, which carries the weight of age-old knowledge and the weight of duty that accompanies unimaginable authority.

As Malkia addresses the assembly, their shape changes, illuminating the room with a soothing light. "Well-being," they said, "is the axis upon which the multiverse spins. Yet, how do we define a state that must be universally applicable and yet, individually experienced?"

An intergalactic representative from a world where bio-harmonic technology is king speaks up, their speech a medley of natural and synthetic sounds. "Well-being for my people is the resonance of life with technology. But what of the universes where silicon and soul are yet to meet? How do we bridge such a vast chasm of experience?"

A sentient machine, its intricate wiring a web of light and quantum circuits, replies. "In the realm of pure information, well-being is the absence of corruption, the perfect flow of data. But we cannot ignore the entropic decay inherent in physical realities. Must we not, therefore, consider destruction as a form of well-being for some?"

The implications of each viewpoint race through Aluta's thoughts as he listens attentively. With a calm demeanour, he advances. "In the Orca Roads, I have witnessed the birth of stars and the silence of voids.

Is the destruction of a dying star not the birthplace of new worlds? Can we not find well-being in the cycle of existence itself?"

The next speaker is someone who looks like a live embodiment of nothingness, the abyss. "To know, we must first embrace ignorance. The void is as much a teacher as the star. Must our well-being not encompass the darkness as well as the light?"

As they ponder Aluta's remarks, the council enters a reflective stillness. Here, in the conversation of opposites, the difficulty of describing universal well-being becomes clear. When their universes are so fundamentally distinct from one another, is it possible for there to be a global standard?

As the council's energy pulses to the beat of the multiverse, Malkia floats above them. "Perhaps our understanding of well-being is not a line but a circle. In every act of creation, there lies the seed of destruction, and in every end, the promise of a new beginning."

The wisdom of Malkia's words resonates with their different views, and the assembly nods in collective accord. The task at hand is to discover a meaning of well-being that pays homage to the one-of-a-kind interplay between creation and emptiness throughout the multiversal fabric.

Upon considering his duty as a Guardian, Aluta discerns the veracity of the council's argument. "The Orca Roads," he exclaims, "are the embodiment of balance. They exist between the realms, belonging to neither and both. Perhaps our well-being lies in the journey, not the destination."

The metaphor of the voyage as a condition of balance, which Aluta used, is something the council members give some thought to. This equilibrium is not static, but rather dynamic and ever flowing, like the cosmic rivers that Aluta protects.

Disputes arose between a number of delegates during the course of the Council of Wellness's deliberations as they pertained to the distribution of resources across their interconnected multiversal realms. Anger flared up as the Brylian Confederacy harvested too much solar plasma from nearby systems.

The Farians sprang into action, their feathers wagging, shouting, "Your actions risk destabilising our stars!" forcibly. "We have raised this exploitation repeatedly to no avail. When will you curb your limitless consumption?"

Ves, the First Chancellor of the Brylians, was responding anxiously from inside his levitation tank, his transparent figure writhing in frustration. "Do not overexaggerate, Farians. Our energy needs are insignificant percentagewise. You assault us over practically non-existent issues."

Malkia stepped in with an authoritative and compassionate voice as tempers flared. "Friends, scarce resources frequently breed such conflicts, but rancour solves naught. I encourage all impacted parties to convene separately and address distribution solutions agreeable to all."

Mediation and mild reprimands helped calm things down. However, even among highly developed races, Aluta was aware that the paradox of infinity would give rise to arguments due to the abundance of unexplored possibilities it contained. It was everyone's responsibility to be firm in their equilibrium-oriented principles and rein in their reactive emotions.

It is becoming more apparent that the pursuit of global harmony is a dynamic endeavour as the debate over competing theories persists. Each dimension of well-being reflects a different universe or reality, and the council agrees that this is the case.

At the end of the session, everyone agrees to keep digging, to learn as much as they can from the multiverse, and to come up with their own unique definition of wellness, one that is both universal and specific, a harmony that respects the interplay between form and void, creation and destruction, knowledge and ignorance.

On this, the second day of the grand council, where the threads of all universes converge, the idea of wellbeing expands into boundless complexity. As protectors of the purity of their own realms, the delegates must now decide how to act in the interest of the whole without compromising the complex web of life that exists throughout all possible realities.

Addressing the assembly, Malkia embodies the shades of worry. "Our goal is universal well-being, yet we stand at a crossroads where one universe's prosperity could be the undoing of another. How do we navigate this delicate balance?"

Aluta advances, his posture betraying the knowledge he has gained from his travels. "In my travels across the Orca Roads, I have seen how the actions in one universe ripple across others. Well-being cannot be a zero-sum game where the advancement of one comes at the cost of another."

"Our advancements have the potential to uplift less developed realms. But how do we share our knowledge without overshadowing their own paths to enlightenment?" asks a representative from a powerful universe that relies on technology.

replied Aluta, "True well-being fosters growth without dependency. It is not about leading them to our light but kindling their own."

Throughout the discussion on multiversal ethics, Aluta's viewpoint stands out as a voice of reason. "Each universe is a note in the symphony of existence. To maintain harmony, we must ensure that every note is allowed to resonate with its own timbre."

A council member, representing the core of a universe with less technological advancement, raises their voice. "We seek not charity but equity. The council must serve as the guardians of a balance that enables all to flourish independently."

As their lights dance across the room, Malkia gives a knowing nod. "Aluta, your insight has illuminated the path we must tread. We shall establish a multiversal framework that encourages self-determination and prevents exploitation."

Aluta, feeling humble, continues, "As we venture down this path, let us remember that well-being is a journey, not a destination. It is a commitment to uphold the dignity of every universe, to listen and learn from each other, and to forge a future where all can thrive."

The profound impact of Aluta's comments moves the council members, who start to formulate a proclamation that captures their shared goal—a theory that would lead the way for multiversal prosperity.

A number of delegates had doubts about the well-being declaration's practicability throughout its preparation. With no means of administrative enforcement, how could they expect such a diverse alliance of civilizations to obey universally?

With a gentle nod, Malkia recognised the doubt. "Enforcement has always been more aspiration than assurance. The declaration serves rather as our collective conscience, reminding all delegates of the sacred responsibility our capabilities place upon us towards less powerful realms."

They took stock of the abruptly reflective audience. "True authority comes not through aggressive checks but self-restraint. We must be our own humble watchmen, vigilant against any perceived exception that violates established principles. That is the deeper purpose here."

A chorus of approval greeted their revelation. The declaration, in Aluta's view, was most powerful when it called for the internal development of an ethical temperament rather than the imposition of artificial external rules. Indeed, self-mastery, not punitive deterrents, was the source of true authority.

The time has come to confirm their shared destiny. The historic pronouncement of the Declaration of Multiversal Well-being is an opportunity for each representative, a voice for their universe, to take part. With the solemnity of the moment hanging in the air, the room descended into a respectful silence.

Malkia motions for the beginning, her light bright and hopeful. "Let us now, together, voice our covenant for the ages."

The first to ascend is a revered being from a bygone era, whose voice reverberates like the earliest stars. "We, the entities and civilizations of the Multiverse, in recognition of our shared existence and interconnected destinies across the vast tapestry of realities, hereby establish this Declaration of Multiversal Well-being. This document signifies our collective commitment to the sustainability, harmony, and flourishing of all forms of life and existence within the Multiverse."

Section One: Recognising Multiversal Diversity

The emissary of a burgeoning culture keeps on, their speech a tune of ambition. "Acknowledge the immense diversity of life, consciousness, and cultures across the Multiverse, and affirm the intrinsic value of all forms of existence. Commit to respecting the unique qualities and needs of each universe, ensuring that actions taken in one universe do not adversely affect the well-being of entities in another."

Section Two: Responsible and Ethical Management

The robotic being from a galaxy of stars and circuits continues the recitation, their computer-generated voice carrying the gravity of their statements. "Uphold the highest standards of ethical conduct in all interactions within the Multiverse, recognising the profound impact our actions have on the collective whole. Ensure responsible stewardship of resources, energy, and knowledge, promoting sustainable practices that benefit all universes."

Section Three: Justice and Equity

The next speaker is a representative from a realm where fluid shapes and dynamic equilibrium predominate. "Strive for equity and fairness in the distribution of resources and opportunities across the

Multiverse. Work to prevent exploitation, oppression, or harm to any beings, regardless of their level of advancement or origin."

Section Four: Maintenance of Independence and Individuality

With the weight of the Orca Roads' heritage, Aluta firmly states the following principle. "Respect the autonomy and self-determination of all entities, ensuring that the collective actions of civilizations do not override individual or cultural identities. Support the right of each universe and its inhabitants to maintain their historical, cultural, and environmental heritage."

Section Five: Working Together in Harmony

An interuniversal peacekeeper makes a solemn vow to "Foster a spirit of cooperation and peaceful coexistence among all entities of the Multiverse. Establish and maintain multiversal channels of communication, diplomacy, and conflict resolution."

Section Six: Promoting Greater Understanding and Knowledge

A representative of a Lumina universe proclaims, "Promote the advancement of knowledge and understanding across the Multiverse, encouraging the free exchange of ideas and information. Support educational and cultural exchanges that enrich the experiences of all multiversal entities."

Section Seven: Dedication to Multiversal Well-being

With their powerful voice, Malkia ends the proclamation. "Dedicate ourselves to the continuous improvement of the well-being of all entities within the Multiverse. Establish and adhere to shared principles and guidelines that ensure the longevity, harmony, and prosperity of the Multiverse."

Standing as one, the congregation listens to the last words. "This Declaration of Multiversal Well-being is a testament to our collective commitment to a future where all forms of life and existence in the Multiverse can thrive in harmony. It is our hope that this document serves as a guiding light for current and future generations, fostering a legacy of respect, cooperation, and mutual prosperity across all realities."

By signing the proclamation, the representatives of the Multiversal Entities pledge to keep these principles, assuring future generations that the multiverse will be a harmonious and balanced environment for all.

A charter for all time, the Declaration resounds to the ends of the universe as a symbol of solidarity and optimism. Standing tall in the waning light, Aluta's figure carries the burden of the council's judgements on his shoulders.

With their intensity reduced to a gentle murmur, Malkia approaches him. "Guardian, your contributions have woven into the very fabric of this declaration. The multiverse is in your debt."

Aluta nods, showing his acceptance and humility. "It was my honour, but the Orca Roads call to me. My journey continues."

Chapter 15
The Creation Council

Where the destiny of emerging cosmoses is precariously poised lies the chamber of the Council of Universal Creation, a meeting place for transcendent minds. In this place, among powerful beings, the story of creation plays out as the stars are born.

From the depths of space-time, the entity known as Jaja rumbles their voice, whose presence vacillates between the visible and invisible worlds. "We stand at the precipice of creation, holding the threads of new universes in our grasp. Yet, with such power comes a question of stewardship. Shall we democratise this divine capability, or shall we guard it jealously, a privilege of the few?"

A delegate whose very being appears to be knit into the fabric of space and time responds with a harmonious melody. "To create is to be godlike. Yet, every star we ignite, every world we mould, every life we potentially foster—must be a testament to our collective will, not just a display of our might."

Using the building blocks of planets that have not yet formed, an entity gives their ideas form. "The democratisation of creation carries the risk of chaos. Without a unified vision, without a consensus of purpose, we risk birthing universes devoid of harmony. Our creations must be a reflection of our most profound unity."

With his experience of the Orca Roads and his insight into the inner workings of both young and old cosmoses, Aluta brings a level-headed perspective to the table. "In the journey through the Orca Roads, I have learned that creation is not just a matter of power, but of purpose. Each universe must be more than a mere experiment; it must be a legacy of our highest aspirations."

A hush of agreement fills the room, as if carried on a cosmic breeze. Every one of the entities understands the gravity of their next actions as guardians of the fires of creation. They have the power to build universes that are ripe with possibilities for art, history, and life—canvases for the greatest tale ever told.

As the Council of Universal Creation moulds the spirit of their sacred mission, the discussion rages on, a tango of ideas and opportunities. As they proclaim, "As architects of realms, we stand divided," Jaja's figure glistens with the promise of worlds yet to be born. "Our unity frays at the edges, as we ponder the nature of the universes we yearn to create. Shall we proceed as a monolith, or shall we celebrate our diversity through the tapestries of distinct realities?"

A harmonious blend of disagreement and consensus fills the room, as if carried by a gentle breeze. An entity, its light reminiscent of a quasar, raises its voice. "To impose a singular principle upon all creation is to stifle the very essence of innovation. Let each of us forge a universe in our image, within the bounds of our understanding, and let diversity be our guiding star."

A being whose shape is a complex web of dark matter, warns against hasty judgement. "Diversity invites chaos. Without a universal framework, we risk the harmony of the multiverse. Our creations must be bound by a code, a covenant that ensures the safety of all."

Each member of the council passionately defends their theory of cosmic creation as the council devolves into heated debate. Aluta observes the passionate conversation and decides to intervene. "I have seen the beauty of variety and the chaos it can birth. Might we not find a middle path? Grant freedom within a framework, allowing for individual expression while safeguarding the collective?"

A settlement is taking shape as a consensus is emerging. "Let us each birth a universe," Jaja said, "defined by our unique laws and visions. But let us also bind ourselves to an accord: should any creation threaten the fabric of the multiverse, we shall unite to restore balance."

With this pact in place, the beings are getting ready to start their great experiment, in which they will each become the creator of a universe and the ruler of a specific reality. With a covenant of mutual guardianship binding them to their fellows, they recognise a common fate and pledge to protect the multiverse's fabric.

There is a buzz in the air, a charge of possibilities about to burst forth. In the heart of this immense gathering, devices and systems engineered to construct a universe from the primordial ooze of potential hum to life, technologies that go beyond understanding.

Jaja starts the creation sequence with their form now steady as reality's foundation. They say, "Let us begin," and the room fills with the glow of creation as a result.

As one by one, the beings make their way to a console and they start the creative incantation, which is a symphony of energy brought together by purpose and intelligence. A concentrated beam of the council's will slices through the void's curtain.

Unbridled creative impulses burst forth in spectacular displays as the vacuum quivered. Whole cosmologies came tumbling into existence, their dynamics and symmetries mirroring the emotive colour palettes of the gods who designed them.

A new universe formed from an endless web of possible wave functions, with particles entangled in probabilistic tensors and squirming under the weight of multiple quantum states. The Ginja combulust gave birth to a violent universe that was a product of viral eruptions and exploding supernovae; this multiverse was passionate and unrelenting in its destruction and reformation cycles.

Intricate mathematical singularities supported tranquil universes that revolved around concepts instead of stars, and the diversity's vastness astounded Aluta. From an endless source of creative energy, every god creates new worlds, whether it is the curving design of Brane plateaus or the higher Hilbert spaces where life thrives.

The assembly witnessed Reality herself bring forth a new multiverse imbued with her mind so that its inhabitants could dwell for all time as worlds beyond worlds spread at a dizzying rate. Her progeny awoke with their minds pre-wired for intellectual inquiry rather than material progress.

Amaterast was the expression on Aluta's face. He sees the black hole quiver before exploding into a rainbow of hues, the very beginning of the cosmos taking a breath. Nebulae dance with light and dust, stars burst like cosmic fireflies, and galaxies take shape before his eyes.

When some universes exploded into existence, it was like a symphony of perfect order; when others came into being, it was more like a wild cacophony of chance and disorder. The dawn of a new cosmos brings with it the pulsating cadence of life and the grave quiet of unrealized possibility.

As these new places take shape, Aluta feels a deep affinity for this creative moment, as if it were a whispered recollection of his own origins. While uttering the words, he becomes engrossed in the grandeur of the scene. "I am witness to the sublime," he breathes.

The room becomes silent as the final universe forms. Each member of the council sees their job as contributing to a constellation of new realities, and they all have their own destinies. An emotional Aluta realises that he has witnessed something very few people ever see: the intentional construction of reality itself, a demonstration of the authority and duty of individuals who dare to pretend to be gods.

"We have not just expanded possibilities but also our responsibilities," Jaja admonished the celestial parents as they marvelled at their creations. "Universes cannot run unchecked. However, paternalistically censoring every quantum event would negate our creative energies."

After some quiet contemplation, they proposed a pact to establish universally applicable humanitarian standards free from dictatorial control. The gods grudgingly consented, with a few, like the goddess of necessary destruction Kali, fighting against any limitations placed on their progeny's universes.

"Reality festers without renewal," she snarled fiercely. Jaja was insistent, hand-crafted precautions necessary, and said, "Who are you to dictate how my works rejuvenate themselves?" "I will follow your advice, Jaja. But watch out, no budding universe thrives under overly controlling authorities," Kali declared with a hint of grovelling.

The result was an uncomfortable harmony, but additional hasty negotiations were certain if Jaja had any inkling of how quickly certain gods turned creative liberties into totalitarian control over new forms of life in other universes. Divine hands had just primed an endless canvas to welcome life's future experiments, and it lay there waiting.

The freshly created worlds' pulsating centres of life become more intricate as they develop. The beings that made everything watch helplessly as sentient beings develop intellect, emotion, and culture, eventually blossoming into complex societies with their own mythologies, histories, and philosophies.

A civilisation of highly evolved beings, academics, and scientists begins to shed light on the secrets of their existence in one such universe. Their hunger for knowledge compels them to explore the boundaries of their reality. While on this never-ending journey, they discover something so massive that it could destroy their entire worldview: their entire cosmos, with all its complexity and breadth, is a fabrication, a product of beings from another dimension.

All through their civilization, this revelation causes a wave of shock and amazement. Some people feel a profound feeling of cosmic enlightenment when they hear the news, and they choose to adore their creators as if they were gods who gave their lives meaning and purpose. They unite as Believers, who regard this finding as a gateway to a more profound comprehension of reality and life.

On the flip side, sentiments of manipulation and betrayal give rise to a rebel faction. Not gods in their eyes, but masterminds behind a massive illusion that has kept them mired in a scripted life, that is how they perceive their creators. The Rebels doubt their own existence, the veracity of their experiences, and the power of their own choice.

A raging inferno of existential dread engulfs humanity as philosophical and ethical disputes flare up. Determinism, consciousness, and the ethics of creation are the revolving doors of the conversation. As a result of this ideological schism, people start to question their own identity and the motives of their unseen makers, which can lead to social instability.

The Council of creators, meantime, are dealing with the fallout from their massive experiment. As the sentient beings they created grapple with the realisation of their own artificiality, they observe with a mix of worry and intrigue.

A heated argument starts. Some people think their creations need assistance, a helping hand, to get through this chaotic discovery. They contend that it would be unethical to abandon their sentient creations to their own devices.

True development and insight, according to these proponents of the non-interference principle, must originate from inside. They hold the view that becoming involved would further strip these beings of their agency, making them feel like they are just pawns in a cosmic drama.

With each passing day, the creators are more and more compelled to face the implications of their deeds, the ethical dilemmas of playing god, and the unanticipated results of introducing consciousness and life into their worlds. It is a striking monument to the power and burden of creation that their creations' fate is hanging in the balance.

Within the majestic halls of the Council of Universal Creation, the balance of cosmic power is finely balanced, as the Creators gather to decide the destiny of worlds. The entities, masters of universes and fate-weavers, have come together to face a problem of unparalleled magnitude: their creations have cried out, seeking knowledge that may set them free or tie them down.

Jaja summons the council to a meeting. "Our creations now gaze upon us, their creators," they proclaim, their voice resonating like a faraway starlit night. "They seek answers, and in doing so, challenge the very nature of our experiment."

The voice of an ethereal entity rises over the uproar as their body radiates with the vitality of a million suns. "We are at a turning point," they proclaim. "To reveal ourselves, to step into their worlds as gods or guardians, is to forever alter their path. Yet, to remain hidden, to deny them the truth, is to consign them to an existence of uncertainty and doubt."

As a figure from a universe where a rebellion has broken out talks, their presence creates a whirlwind of dark matter, the debate heats up. "My universe teeters on the brink of chaos. The factions born from our revelation threaten to tear apart the fabric of their society. Perhaps it is time to close the curtain on this grand play."

In response, another being a composite of quantum threads proposes a picture of harmony. "To extinguish their existence would be an act of cosmic cruelty. We must embrace our role as guardians, guiding them towards a future where they can flourish, even amidst the knowledge of their origins."

An entity whose universe gave rise to a group of believers now raises a voice of disagreement. "Why not ascend to our rightful place as their deities? They look to us for guidance, for purpose. We could shepherd them towards greatness."

The council is stuck; their decision will have consequences that reach into the universe. As he speaks from his journey's wisdom, Aluta in the middle of this discussion. "In my travels, I have learned that the greatest gift we can offer is not control but understanding. Our creations deserve to forge their path, with or without our direct intervention. To be a true guardian is to empower, not to enslave or extinguish."

The room goes quiet as everyone thinks about what Aluta said. The council faces a critical decision: either emerge from the shadows as gods and guardians or remain in the background and let their creations fend for themselves. Their choice will have far-reaching consequences, influencing not just the destiny of their virtual worlds but also their very being as creators.

With a profound solemnity, Jaja reveals the council's choice, encapsulating their united resolve. "We shall reveal ourselves to our creations, not as deities to be worshipped, but as guardians to guide and support. We shall honour their autonomy, their right to exist and evolve, as we offer our wisdom."

An extraordinary event that goes beyond worlds and realities is about to take place: the gathering of creators and their works. As the creatures pass the threshold of their own universes, the inhabitants of these manufactured worlds respond in a wide range of ways, including amazement, scepticism, curiosity, and even dread.

The entities and their creatures square off in a massive assembly where the atmosphere is electric with revelation. Asking questions like, "Why were we created? What is our purpose? Do we have free will, or are we just puppets in your grand design?" The makers listen, realising the profound existential crisis their discoveries have caused.

Jaja gives a speech to the audience. "You were created not as an experiment in vanity, but as an expression of our quest to understand existence. Your purpose is your own to define. We bestow upon you the gift of knowledge, the freedom to explore your potential, and the assurance that you are not alone in this vast cosmos."

A tapestry of mutual respect and understanding is the meeting's resolution. Feeling awed by the profound awareness they have brought into the world, the creators solemnly promise to take on the role of guardians, offering guidance when necessary while perpetually recognising the inherent autonomy of their works. In exchange, the beings residing in these virtual worlds have shown an eagerness to accept and even welcome their newfound guardianship, eager to learn and develop under their watchful eyes.

With the assembly's departure, a fresh era in the annals of the universe commences. Now that the artificial worlds know where they came from, they can go out on a path of self-discovery with the help of beings that have evolved beyond their original creator roles to become guides, teachers, and friends. Aluta, the Orca Roads Guardian, stands among them, content in the knowledge that his cosmic odyssey has contributed to the development of this mutually beneficial relationship between beings of the Universe and their works of art.

"Regarde, Q," X starts, their voice a beautiful medley of the otherworldly and the profound, "this moment is a dance of creation and understanding, a ballet of existence itself. The universes, with all their complexities, have found harmony in the revelation of truth. It is a celestial symphony, n'est-ce pas?"

A deep nod is the response from Q, whose very being is a thread in the tapestry of quantum realities. "Indeed, X. It is a convergence of possibilities, a testament to the multiverse's infinite tapestry. The interaction between creators and their creations, it is not just a meeting—it is an exchange of fundamental understandings, a merging of perspectives across dimensions."

After X takes one last look around the gathering, they shift their focus to the Orca Roads. "Aluta, mon ami, continues to be the bridge between worlds, the guardian of dynamic balance. His path is one of constant discovery, an eternal voyage through the heart of existence."

Chapter 16
Verse of Mortal Liberation

Once Aluta makes it to the Type 16 Civilization on his cosmic voyage, he finds that the idea of death is a thing of the past. As he watches, the Eternal Society comes into view, a symbol of the highest level of scientific and philosophical achievement. Residents here seem to have escaped the clutches of death and the passage of time altogether.

Aluta meets Kwame, a philosopher and historian entirely absorbed in the study of ancient civilizations, as he makes his way across this realm of eternal life. Because of his inquisitive mind and tendency towards introspection, Kwame spends a lot of time poring over historical documents, trying to piece together how different cultures' views on mortality have influenced their communities.

He thinks about how people have always sought significance in life and sought to leave a lasting legacy because of the certainty of death. When compared to the Eternal Society's view of life as a never-ending adventure, Aluta finds Kwame's exploration fascinating.

Through his examination of several cultural perspectives on mortality, Kwame raised important issues about the existential effects of near-immortality. Was death really the impetus for creativity, significance, and the very soul of man? On the other hand, was that just an excuse for the ultimate injustice of needless deaths?

He started writing experimental philosophical tracts in which he asked the unthinkable: were the benefits of immortality greater than the insights one would get from accepting death? Kwame was well aware that he was jeopardising thousands of years of religious dogma that had provided comfort in the face of impermanence. However, his culture now had the means to make death unnecessary.

"Through wresting away death's power we gained scientific mastery but perhaps lost some ineffable psychic quality," he wrote in secret. It is death itself that brings a life to a close, according to philosophers who have written about the need to be ready for the last trip. Is this the end of an era of immortals, or are we free to roam?

Selene, a famous architect who stunned her contemporaries by choosing euthanasia at the end of a long and distinguished life, provided unexpected validation for his findings. She thanked Kwame for bringing her to a realisation in her goodbye note. "Immortality strips life of savour by removing the bookends of existence."

Her daring moves infuriated conservatives and gave reformers a boost in their fight for controlled death options. Unintentionally, Kwame became the leader of a rising philosophical rebellion as cultural conflicts over death's place in their society escalated and more turmoil over existential freedom emerged.

In addition to existentialist concerns about his own existence, he also wondered about the nature and purpose of the universe as a whole. He echoes the societal unconscious as he wonders, "What is the meaning of life when death is no longer its inevitable conclusion?"

The idea of life's sacredness is difficult for Kwame to fathom in a culture where death is never a consideration. He thinks on the moral implications of creating and destroying life in a cosmos where the natural order of things has been upset. "Should we, as immortal beings, be shielded from death at all costs, protected from external threats as well as our internal conflicts?" As the starry sky beyond his window expands, Kwame finds himself immersed in thought.

Kwame chooses to make public his observations out of a desire to impart wisdom and stimulate discussion. In "What the Life," a collection of essays and conversations, he makes his ideas publicly available. A heated discussion breaks out among the Eternal Society members in response to these articles. Kwame's views make them question their entire existence and make them rethink what it means to live and die.

Deepening his exploration of these existential questions forces Kwame to face the tension between independence and accountability. Given their near immortality, he wonders if the Eternal Society members should have more freedom to choose their own fates or if they need more care and supervision due to their immortality.

The search for solutions that Kwame undertakes mirrors the collective consciousness of the Eternal Society. His investigations and contemplations spark a larger conversation inside the society, as its members start to question their views on mortality, meaning of life, and the universe as a whole.

"What the Life" has a divided reception from the general population. Concerned that challenging the worth of their immortality would cause anarchy and existential crises, some members of society see Kwame's ideas as an affront to the current system. Their victory over death, they say, is something to be proud of, not questioned.

Contrarily, an expanding group regards Kwame's ideas as liberating. They are open to the thought that learning about death and its function in history can help them better appreciate their present-day near-immortality. In a universe where death is a faraway notion, this group perceives Kwame's art as a chance to delve into the profound implications of life.

In the middle of all this intellectual upheaval, Aluta talks to both sides, sharing his experience as a guardian who has travelled the Orca Roads. To provide further perspective and depth to the continuing conversation, he shares thoughts from cultures that have struggled with existence, mortality, and all in between.

Beyond its initial philosophical intent, Kwame's "What the Life" develops into a socially charged introspection that prompts the Eternal Society's inhabitants to reconsider their conception of immortality by investigating age-old existential questions.

The struggle over Kwame's philosophical investigations hits a crossroads in the middle of the Eternal Society. Seeing the social turmoil first-hand, Aluta seeks out Kwame to gain a better grasp of the situation. They discuss the complexities of life, death, and the freedom to choose one's own fate in a talk that is full of insight and understanding.

At the same time, this whirlwind has thrust the knowledgeable and ancient people that make up the civilization's governing council squarely in its path. Is it morally acceptable to allow their population to terminate their everlasting lives? This is a very serious matter. It is an existential question that goes to the heart of their society's principles.

As the council weighed the gravity of legalizing death among their immortal population, Chief Ethicist Isa stood, his expression grave.

"I must voice strong objection to this proposal," he began. "Suicide among immortal beings violates fundamental moral codes. To endorse it would undo millennia of societal evolution."

Murmurs rippled through the chamber, but Isa continued undeterred. "We sought immortality to liberate sentient life from oblivion. How can we ethically then facilitate access to that same abyss? To us, death holds no organic purpose as natural biological law."

"Our physiology no longer binds us to mortality. Thus, seeking death among us is itself an aberration, indicating mental imbalance or delusion." Isa activated neurological scans showing suicide increased alpha wave incoherence. "Indeed, organic suicidal impulses derive from temporary chemical imbalances correctable through our medical science."

The rending anguish on the Andromedans' faces flashed in Isa's mind, steeling his resolve. "We cannot enable what our entire society strives to prevent – the permanent destruction of a thinking being's continuity. Life is an irreplaceable gift, one far too precious to surrender to fleeting despairs."

He straightened; hands clasped with conviction behind his back. "I say this not to punish but protect, as shielding misguided minds from irreversible errors they will regret once their psyches are restored. If we are to remain true to our convictions, compassion obliges us to refuse this right to die."

Isa afforded the council a deep nod before resuming his seat. "Immortality must signify life undefeasible. We failed those already lost; let us not fail those still dwelling in darkness needing our light."

The council agrees to temporarily restrict Kwame's writings in an effort to calm the escalating tension as the argument continues to flare. The censoring does not stop Kwame, though; he finds a way to distribute his ideas through other blockchain networks. This way, his message will keep getting out to people. His works, which are today both more accessible and harder to pin down, represent defiance and independent thinking.

Arresting Kwame in an effort to rein on his rising prominence just makes matters worse. His detention makes him an even more powerful symbol of existential freedom, and his message becomes even more widely disseminated. Once heard only in philosophical circles, Kwame's ideas are now resonating throughout the Eternal Society's streets and online forums.

Kwame struggles with inner turmoil while confined to his prison cell. An introspective quest, his philosophical exploration of mortality forces him to rethink his own existence and the decisions he has made. In a culture where dying is taboo, he wonders what it means to be alive.

The council fiercely debated legalizing death among immortals, Aluta stepped forward, his expression thoughtful.

"While immortality liberates from oblivion, it also carries the duty not to mandate continued existence for all," he began gently. Isa bristled but Aluta raised a conciliatory hand.

"Without the freedom to choose their own path, some may suffer silently, believing unaware that alternatives exist to their despair. Might granting this right enable them to voice inner torments long suppressed?"

Several delegates nodded slowly as Aluta continued. "Autonomy over one's fate is no trivial matter. You cannot discern all those quietly yearning for escape unless they can openly seek it without shame. Provide liberty, and you may uncover who requires your compassion most."

Isa stood abruptly, face tense with frustration. "And if we validate the option of suicide, do we not strengthen its seduction for fragile minds that might otherwise endure?"

Aluta weighed the statement thoughtfully before replying. "Perhaps, but perhaps not. We must have faith that life's allure remains the stronger. Offer them only open ears, hearts free from judgment, and hands to grasp for stability."

As the vociferous debates concluded, an anonymous vote was held on permitting voluntary suicide under strict assessment. The verdict narrowly passed in favour of Aluta's stance, swayed by his call for wisdom and empathy when confronting an issue involving such existentially conflicting views.

Isa acquiesced reluctantly, inwardly fearing the policy would only add to future regret and tragedy. But the council's majority believed that forbidding personal autonomy, even over mortality, violated ethical principles of freedom and consent.

The news shakes the Eternal Society to its core. For some, it is finally their right to decide for themselves, and that is a comfort. That they are free to choose their own fate, even if it means ending their endless journey, is something they take as a sign of their uniqueness and autonomy.

Some people are furious and hopeless about the decision. To them, it represents giving up to a backwards idea of reality and a rejection of society's basic values. Outrageous arguments and protests break out as people fiercely defend their stances on the value of life and the morality of suicide.

Following his release, Kwame, who has become a symbol of the fight for existential independence within the Eternal Society, does his last and most moving act of protest. A stirring and moving poem capture his life's journey, contemplations of death, and acceptance of his own mortality that he writes.

In this poem, "Last Verse," Kwame declares his newfound comprehension of life and death and becomes his living testament. There is an overwhelming sense of doom in every word he writes. By cleverly tying his vitality to the poetry, Kwame establishes a restriction on the total number of words he will compose. So, his last work is a moving countdown to his own death, since he gets closer to his goal with each word he writes.

"Last Verse
Oh' life let my life bloom and fade,
Oh' freedom today my debt is paid.
Embrace the selves I've cherished and known,
As I dive into the depths of the unknown
Cry if it soothes, for loss carves deep,
But this life was never mines to keep.
Remember me in your jubilant song,
For in your harmony, I'll dance along.
For life, like rivers, must onward flow,
Goodbye friends, and death Hello!"

The poem touches the hearts and thoughts of the citizens of the Eternal Society like a ripple in a quiet pond. Participating in the poetry with a feeling of sombre awe, Kwame's followers embrace his perspective as a way to break free from the shackles of everlasting life. Kwame has decided to accept finality, and for them, every syllable is a shared experience, a communal trip.

An organic whole, "Last Verse" merges art and life. Knowing that Kwame is getting closer to his self-imposed conclusion with every sentence, the residents cling to every word.

The entire society holds its breath as Kwame writes his last word. The poet keeps his word after using up all of his self-allocated vocabulary. His death becomes more than a private act of closure; it becomes a social event, a watershed moment that tests the eternal society's view of mortality.

The impact of Kwame's death on the community will last forever. The poem he wrote bears witness to his bravery and the intellectual impact he had. It is a constant reminder of the preciousness of existence, the finality of death, and the freedom that each individual has to chart their own course through the endless reaches of space and time.

Aluta experiences profound introspection. "Kwame's choice, his last verse, it is a reminder of the ephemeral nature of existence, even in a world where eternity is the norm," he says. "His poem, like a star that burns brightly before fading away, illuminates the value of each moment, each choice we make in the cosmic dance of life and death."

"Ah, Kwame, un poète de l'éternité, il an opté pour l'éternité et a laissé son existence à son gré," X explains "The thoughts he left behind will reverberate through time and space, serving as a constant reminder that life without meaning is meaningless existence."

The more profound ramifications are considered by Q. "The social turmoil that Kwame's decision sparked is a perfect illustration of the delicate equilibrium between being and not being. The decision he made to terminate his eternal quest collapsed all choices into one clear course of action; it was a quantum event in and of itself."

Each member of the trio is deep in thought, yet they are bound together by the common experience of seeing a civilisation struggle with one of the most fundamental questions of being.

Chapter 17
Prelude to Oblivion

Every thread of reality in the multiverse was bracing for a tempest, a conflict that would tear the cosmic fabric apart. The participants, who ranged in shape and philosophy, got ready for battle, each with their own agenda, oblivious to the potential repercussions of their deeds.

A realm known as Tzarith

The Tzariths were an energy-based civilisation that harnessed the light from the stars. They were able to transform gravitational forces into lethal weapons because of the technology they developed. Believing in their mission to expand their dominance over the multiverse, they prepared for battle with a serious grasp of its gravity.

The Group Known as Cygnus

The Cygnus Collective, an AI-driven civilization that had surpassed material forms, saw the approaching conflict as an essential computational calculation. The quantum weapons at their disposal may destroy matter itself. But they failed to see the unpredictable anarchy of battle because they relied too much on reasoning and probability calculations.

The Hive of Aruk

The Aruk were experts in biological warfare; they were insectoid entities who operated as one collective consciousness. Toxins that could change their enemies' genetic composition were part of their preparations. These biological agents could induce mutations that could backfire and pose new dangers to their ranks.

An Alliance of Xelarians

Defence was the primary priority of the Xelarians, a federation of multiple humanoid races. They constructed walls that extended across dimensions to protect their domains. While their cautious strategy was well-intentioned and meant to safeguard their kingdoms, the excessive energy consumption of these barriers threatened their own survival.

Monks from Oronthos

The Oronthos were highly spiritual beings that yearned for peace and tranquilly. But the impending danger of battle drove them to create psychic weapons that could render their opponents helpless by injecting them with an overpowering sense of existential dread. Despite not being fatal, this strategy ran the danger of releasing unstoppable mental plagues.

An Enclave in Nebulon

In the shadows, the Nebulons, experts in cunning and stealth, readied themselves for battle. Their ships and armies could evade detection by most sensors including the human eye thanks to their advanced cloaking technology. But technology that could defeat invisibility were able to exploit their over-reliance on stealth.

Engineers from Vortex

As their principal weapon, the Vortex Engineers—a culture that had perfected the art of space and time manipulation—created temporal anomalies. There were dangers to tampering with time, but they could also trap opponents in time loops. Unforeseen consequences for their own chronology can result from paradoxes they created.

Aluta watched the multiverses get ready, and he saw a tangled web of interconnected processes, like a cosmic chess game where every move had unexpected results. There was an extremely precarious power dynamic, with enormously high stakes. An intervening in a conflict with the potential to destroy entire civilizations and the very foundations of reality was something the Orca Roads Guardian felt he had to do. Despite the immense difficulty of the task, Aluta remained steadfast in his pursuit of harmony and equilibrium.

The Grand Chamber of the Central Universe was a tense place as Aluta met with the Grand Master Peacekeeper, a being with aeons of wisdom whose job it was to preserve the multiverse in harmony. Here in this solemn room, Aluta hoped to unravel the knot of causes and effects that had brought about this impending disaster.

"Guardian," the Grand Master started, his voice dripping with unspoken sorrows, "the beginning of this imminent war is based on greed and dread. A faction, possessed of an insatiable desire for power, sought to increase their sphere of influence by focusing on lesser universes, claiming they were doing it in the name of unity and protection."

The cosmic tapestry that adorned the chamber's walls told tales of triumph and tragedy, and Aluta's eyes mirrored this. He listened carefully.

"Their actions," said the Grand Master, "ignited a chain reaction. Other multiverses, sensing a shift in the delicate balance of power, fortified their defences. This escalation sparked a resource crisis, as the demand for materials to build weapons and shields soared, depleting reserves and igniting fierce competition."

The realisation of the vicious cycle began to weigh heavily on Aluta's heart. "And this competition has it not threatened the very fabric of peace we have so painstakingly woven?"

"Indeed, Guardian," the Grand Master said, his intense stare cutting through the fabric of space and time. "The ambition of a few now risks unravelling the peacekeeping efforts of the collective. Our interventions, once a beacon of stability, now stand on the precipice of irrelevance as mistrust and fear overshadow our call for unity."

Standing there, Aluta took in the seriousness of the situation. All of the multiverses were at danger from the prospect of such a massive war, not just their own realities. A fragile peace, the product of centuries of diplomatic efforts and mutual understanding, was about to crumble.

As the Guardian of the Orca Roads, Aluta was aware that his trip was about to take a crucial turn, but he was determined to prevent this calamity. Restoring equilibrium and preventing conflict were his twofold objectives.

At the epicentre of the battle, Aluta continued to explore the complex web of political manoeuvring and power struggles that had brought the many universes to the brink of war. In his quest to comprehend the viewpoints behind the impending clash, he journeyed from universe to universe, each a distinct fabric of existence and ideas.

A complex web of anxieties and goals drove the arms race, as he discussed in his conversations:

A belief in their predestined right to govern the multiverse drove the expansionist ambitions of the Tzarith Empire, which he heard about from them. The fact that they were getting ready to fight showed that this was their fate. With a piercing stare, the emperor said, "Our destiny is written in the stars, Aluta. We are born to lead, to expand. It is our right, our duty."

The emperor's clinched hand expressed determination: "In the dance of the cosmos, some must lead while others follow. It is the natural order." Aluta's voice had a hint of melancholy as he said, "But at what cost? Expansion need not be an act of war."

After speaking with members of the Cygnus Collective, he learned that their military readiness was an algorithmic reaction to the impending doom of their civilization. Because conflict is inherently chaotic, their logic-driven approach failed to account for it. The AI ambassador's eyes sparkle and his voice is devoid of emotion as he says, "Our calculations indicate a high probability of conflict. We prepare as logic dictates." Aluta leans forward, truly believing, "Can logic not find a path to peace?" The AI Ambassador responds, "Peace is an ideal state, yet the variables of free will create unpredictability."

Aluta revealed the Hive's dread of genetic destruction in their conversation, which prompted them to create powerful biochemical weapons for self-defense. Aluta calmly tries to reason: "Survival need not mean the destruction of others." The Hive Mind surges defensively, echoing: "In nature, there is always a predator and prey. We choose not to be the latter." So, "Our survival is paramount. We develop what we must to protect the hive."

The Xelarian Alliance maintained that their guarded stance stemmed from a conservative, protectionist ideology. They spent a lot of money protecting their worlds since Aluta could feel their terror of invasion and collapse. Aluta asks with a glimmer of optimism, "Is there room for trust in your philosophy?" The Councillor sighs, almost resigned, "Trust is a luxury in a universe where war looms." The Councillor adopts a cautious expression and says, "We fortify because we value life. Our barriers are shields, not swords."

The Oronthos Monks' movement from pacifism to the creation of mental weaponry piqued Aluta's interest. Their goal in making this change was to defend their culture from outside threats without killing anyone. Serenely, the monk said, "We seek balance, Aluta. Even in war, we search for a path that avoids bloodshed."

Asking with a twinkle in his eye, Aluta motivated: "Can your path influence others to seek peace?"

Meditating monk says, "We can only hope our actions resonate."

The Nebulon Enclave's cultural emphasis on subtlety and surprise gave rise to its dependence on stealth as a tactic. Their fear of confrontation was something Aluta took note of. As the strategist smirked and waved his finger, he said, "The art of war is in not being there when the strike lands." Aluta furrowed his brow in anxiety, and the strategist responded with a dismissive wave: "Invisibility is our strength. We strike unseen, a ghostly force."

The Vortex Engineers took a revolutionary tack in battle by experimenting with time anomalies. Confidence in their expertise, Aluta realised, was the driving force behind their acts, even if they knew the hazards were there. The engineer boasts with a touch of hubris,

"Our enemies will find themselves lost in an endless loop. We control time itself.".

With a delicate touch, Aluta asks, "Is not there a danger in such power?""

"Power is danger, Aluta," the engineer said with an air of self-assuredness. "Yet it serves as a shield as well."

Aluta discovered that the war preparations of each empire mirrored their innermost desires, fears, and cultural values. This insight deepened his comprehension of the intricate network of causes that might cause a catastrophic interuniversal war. Aluta, resolute in his endeavours, summoned a council of interuniversals at the Capital Universe to try to pass a peace treaty.

As Aluta proposed his peace treaty to the Multiverse Council, tense murmurs rippled through the chamber. He could sense the representatives' scepticism and fear of lost power hanging heavily in the air.

The T'zarith Emperor slammed an energy-wreathed fist onto the table, his aura flaring dangerously. "You expect us to sign away our imperial destiny on mere paper? Never!" he roared. The Cygnus Collective clicked in agreement, their hive mind analysing strategic weaknesses such a treaty would cultivate.

Seeing support for continued war solidifying, Aluta raised his hands diplomatically. "I propose no domination over any realm, only a promise to temper actions for the good of all. Is that not a noble vision?"

"Pretty words hiding cowardice!" the Emperor spat back. "You chain mighty civilizations that should stand glorious against infant races you coddle!" The undercurrent of agreement among other powerful leaders showed Aluta the cracks in unity facing collapse.

His voice resounded through the hall as Aluta stood poised and determined in the magnificent chamber of the Multiverse Council, where the multitude of civilizations converge. "We are at a pivotal moment, where our decisions will shape the cosmos," he said with quiet authority. Come with me on a journey towards peace."

A hush fell over the assembly as he spoke; delegates from many worlds, each with its own set of values and concerns, considered his every word. The T'zarith Emperor continued, "Our destiny is to expand. Treaties alone cannot control the celestial bodies whims". His voice echoed with the force of gravity he controlled.

"Logical frameworks can coexist with expansionist ambitions," the Cygnus AI, a group of highly intelligent artificial intelligences, said with a tone befitting a logical think tank. Their emotionless statements nevertheless carried the weight of reason, and we can move forward without confrontation.

"Our aim is not to bind the stars, but to align them," Aluta told the gathering, sensing the tension in the room and knowing he had to be careful. "We can find guidance in a treaty that honours the hopes of all civilizations and keeps them from going to war. His idea was a ray of hope in the middle of the impending storm of opposition."

For hours, Aluta deftly dispelled doubts, patiently explaining how unchecked expansion risked multiversal instability from resource depletion and internecine conflicts. He highlighted the partnership and prosperity potential through collaboration. Gradually, reluctant delegates reluctantly conceded their projections showed Aluta's wisdom, though bitterness lingered at perceived lost sovereignty.

Finally, the T'zarith Emperor remained the sole holdout glowering behind his ontological shielding. But observing peers' gradual acquiescence, he could not resist the subtly intense peer pressure. With a roar of frustration, the Emperor slammed the treaty in savage concession, his aura promising swift vengeance for this humiliation. The Multiverse Council had spoken, but Aluta wondered whether equilibrium could balance on a peace so reluctantly forged.

One by one, they walked up to the dais, their signatures leaving an imprint on the multiverse. Aluta observed, feeling a mix of relief and accomplishment. The treaty they signed was more than just a document; it was a commitment to maintain peace in a universe filled with ambition and power.

A silent acknowledgement of the impending battle washed over the room as the last signature sealed the deal, and a sigh of relief resounded through the room as the formerly bitter adversaries nodded respectfully to one another.

With a final look at the council, Aluta headed towards the Orca Roads, his heart lifted by the knowledge that peace, fragile but powerful, had been achieved under his guidance. It was a sweet triumph for him, knowing his mission was accomplished but also that his journey was far from over.

The ethereal light cocooned Aluta in the Orca Roads, sweeping him away from the magnificence of the Multiverse Council. In his wake, a smattering of misunderstanding spread like wildfire, and the false rumour of an assault on the capital of the Strategist swept through the multiverses like a tsunami, ripping the delicate peace that Aluta had laboriously woven.

The universe unravelled before Aluta's eyes as he watched in terror as General Hydra, leader of the Nebulon, slayed all the members of the council. Betraying their treaty within seconds of signing under the pretence that her home world had been attacked unexpectedly. The truth was not clear whether Hydra was misinformed or this was always the plan.

This horrific act initiated the multiversal war Aluta had feared. The T'zariths retaliated by sending their planet-sized gravitational wave emitters crashing down on Nebula, destroying fleets and resource nodes that were vital to the Nebulons' intricate defence network.

A million worlds were destroyed in hours by unfathomable weaponry. Entire star clusters were turned into virtual plasma by the Cygnus Collective, wiping out vast swaths of reality. Aggressive nano-swarms devoured biomechanical victims from the inside out.

Some civilizations were ripped apart by genetically modified monsters, while others were reduced to radioactive ruins.

Due to the obliteration of their progenitors in the cross-chronal carnage, future civilizations faded out of probability as the Vortex Engineers entered the fray, rupturing space-time across multiple interacting dimensions. The timestream was ravaged by the cascading annihilation.

At last, there was nothing but emptiness and quiet; the once-mighty nations of the Multiverse were either wiped out or reduced to a motley cast of refugees; the deceit of Hydra had sown the seeds of complete war, and the seeds of total oblivion had grown from those seeds; and the Orca Roads had carried Aluta away before the last catastrophic wavefronts of the temporal weaponry could reach him.

As he sank into a state of horrified contemplation amidst the glowing ruins of those once proud civilizations, he could not help but think about how their ambitious technology had given them the keys to rule the heavens, but how their failure to control their fears and mistrust had unleashed Armageddon instead. It served as a sobering reminder to all who came after that compassion and understanding must rule power, lest power lead to catastrophe.

The multiverses, which had been a beautiful tapestry of peaceful coexistence, were now battlefields of devastating war. The Tzarith Empire distorted space itself with their gravitational pull, while the Cygnus Collective, with pinpoint accuracy, annihilated matter, creating empty spaces where stars had once been.

The Xelarian Alliance, once the last line of defence, collapsed under the relentless attack, their interdimensional barriers breached, as the Aruk Hive unleashed its biochemical weapons, changing the genetic composition of entire species in a twisted dance of evolution and annihilation.

In the heat of battle, the Oronthos Monks sent tidal waves of existential fear crashing into their enemies' heads, rendering them mentally crippled. The masters of stealth, the Nebulon Enclave, launched an assassination attempt, but their opponents had already planned their move.

Attempting to change the course of events, the Vortex Engineers broke the fabric of time itself, leading to paradoxes that warped reality into shapes none could have imagined.

The multiversal conflict was more than simply a clash of civilizations; it was the breakdown of all they had constructed, and Aluta, drifting in the Orca Roads, felt a deep sense of powerlessness as he watched the war he had fought so hard to avoid become a vortex of devastation, devouring everything in its wake.

Due to the released powers that were too enormous for the universe to contain, stars collapsed, galaxies clashed, and entire universes blinked out of existence as the conflict intensified, ripping the fabric of the multiverses apart.

In the middle of this end-of-the-world, Aluta came to terms with the terrible reality: the conflict was inevitable, a great extinction event that would leave behind nothing but the ghosts of long-gone civilizations. He beheld, with a heavy heart, the disintegration of the multiverses he had once marvelled at into cosmic dust and the echoes of long-lost legacies.

Aluta, in the Orca Roads, was unharmed but alone, a sole eyewitness to a cosmic catastrophe: the end of the multiversal conflict that had begun with miscommunication and ended in terror.

With the dying light of the multiverses, Aluta saw the transience of life and the precarious equilibrium that kept the universe together. He had served as protector, mediator, and peacemaker, but now he could only watch as creation crumbled.

Once a thriving tapestry of life and wonder, the multiverse was now a void, a monument to the devastating power of fear and ambition. The Orca Roads, now quiet and solemn, guided Aluta across the remains of what once was.

In this emptiness, Aluta discovered a sorrow-driven determination. He would bear the legacies of the fallen multiverses, the tales of cultures that once fantasised about space travel. And deep within him, he maintained a sliver of optimism, a faith that life would discover a way to start over in some distant corner of the universe.

Chapter 18
Code 17

The Vortex Engineers, who were experts in manipulating space and time, sought refuge in the unexplored dimensions of existence escaping the devastating multiverse war. Unbeknownst to Aluta, who had lamented the seeming complete extinction of life, they flourished in these otherworldly domains.

Feelings of relief and excitement raced through Aluta's heart as he discovered this hidden paradise. It was a revelation that the universe had endured, a glimmer of optimism in what he thought was a completely destroyed scene. The Vortex Engineers had created a society that exemplified perfection in many aspects while also escaping the terrible clutches of the conflict.

The fractal lattices that pulsed with pale violet light adorned every structure and pathway of the Vortex city, which Aluta beheld in crystalline architecture. He observed both the breath-taking beauty and the unsettling homogeneity - all around were the identical harmonic shapes that obscured any discernible cultural or personal characteristics.

It was clear to Aluta that this culture has mastered many of the age-old problems that plague all societies. None of these things existed: hunger, strife, or illness. Still, a tangible feeling of stagnation had resulted from the lack of struggle. The pioneers of space, the once-dynamic Vortex Engineers, now appeared satisfied with just existing, their desire for discovery and invention stifled by the ease of their utopia.

Their obsession with establishing order sapped life of its vital vitality as they sought utopian perfection, which led to a stagnation of their culture. The wonderful, chaotic variety that the multiverse had taken away broke Aluta's heart. Such a cost-free calm was just not worth it. He wondered if was possible to bring back that complex web of extremely unlikely forms of diverse beings and entities, cultures, ideologies, and histories.

Aluta was aware that his idea of restoration was not without its dangers, but he had faith that the rekindled friction between different cultures would serve as a catalyst for progress and strength. Discourse, and often even confrontation, between beings and entities with very different opinions was what gave rise to innovation. The only way for a great thinker to arise is from a chaotic dialectic stew, not from peaceful agreement.

Aluta hesitated as he walked by the main archives, uncertain if he had made too many assumptions. He had no business coming up with such an idea after that disastrous attempt to broker multiversal peace. However, the image of his parents' radiant faces flashed through his thoughts, serving as a reminder that there was more to life than meaningless solace. "Could it be possible for diversity to be born of a monolithic culture as this one?" the Guardian wondered aloud as he braced himself for the memory that would later haunt him.

In Aluta's observations, the Vortex Engineers functioned as a hive mind, with each member contributing to a larger whole. Their sophisticated technology and knowledge of the mind were on full display in this psychological wonder. But there was also a homogeneity of ideas and experiences brought about by this collective awareness. Cultures lacked the colourful tapestry of personal narratives, distinct viewpoints, and cultural diversity that Aluta had long loved.

Aluta could appreciate the allure of such a tranquil life after seeing the devastation that war can wreak and seeing entire universes destroyed. The sacrifices made by the Vortex Engineers left him feeling bereft. Their paradise was peaceful and secure, but it was missing the wild and unpredictable things that, in his view, gave life its real flavour and purpose.

The presence of these towns seemed paradoxical to Aluta as he strolled through them. Many would say the Vortex Engineers had reached the zenith of achievement, but this was not the case instead this was complacency. Peace and security in their utopian hell had come at the expense of originality, diversity, and identity itself.

Aluta saw the Vortex Engineers' paradise as a symbol of the need of maintaining a balance between tyranny and liberty, standardisation and individuality. The story taught us about the difficulties of civilization and how we should never stop striving for a utopia. As he departed from their dimension, cut off from the rest of the universe, he took with him a fresh respect for the uncertain and frequently turbulent path of existence.

The next day, Aluta went to the History of War Museum, where artefacts and exhibits murmured tales of the past. There, he discovered an unusual connection with Jabari, the Guardian. They discussed the competing ideals of Aluta, the futurist, and Jabari, the preserver, committed to protecting the past, in their partnership, which was characterised by courteous argument and intellectual sparring.

The weighty duty of safeguarding the artefacts from long-vanished civilizations fell on Jabari, a person whose very being was intertwined with the museum's fabric. His position was firm: according to the modern Vortex Engineers, these cultures were not only long since vanished, but their whole essence was savage. A digital resurrection prospect, the code 17 multiverse backup belonged to a bygone age that was better left forgotten. There were severe repercussions for even considering getting access to it, since it was considered prohibited.

Jabari's life was like a calm lake until Aluta showed up at the museum. Curiosity about Aluta's otherworldly viewpoint piqued the Jabari's interest, but he was also leery of his revolutionary beliefs. The ethics of resurrection and the significance of diversity in the universe were common philosophical topics of discussion.

Standing before the locked vault housing code 17, Jabari spoke with a heavy dose of caution. "Aluta, to even contemplate the resurrection of these multiverses is to dance on the edge of oblivion. Here, such thoughts are not just heresy—they are a call to destruction."

The potential rewards and threats of what was beyond the vault rushed through Aluta's thoughts. The very thought of bringing the multiverses back to life sparked an innate need in him to make right what had been wrong. Still, he knew full well what may happen if he did that. A return to the multiverse that was once scarred by the conflict could reignite fires that had long since died out.

Jabari kept a sharp eye on Aluta, his stare sharp but not cruel. "Your heart is torn between two realms, Aluta. The future you envision and the past we preserve here are worlds apart. Tread carefully, for the line between restoration and ruin is perilously thin."

At that moment, Aluta understood that Jabari was more than simply a historian; he was also a defender of the delicate equilibrium that the universe had recently accomplished, even though they had fundamentally different viewpoints. Because of their common function as guardians, though of distinct parts of life, Aluta felt a bond with Jabari in that insight.

Aluta wandered the empty halls of the museum alone, his footsteps echoing accusations of failure. The artifacts of extinct civilizations condemned his role in their demise, each silent memorial harder to bear than the last.

Had he ever been the foretold Guardian, or just a fraud doomed to usher in destruction? Aluta's shame and self-doubt festered, his celebrated title now a bitter curse. Sleepless, he plumbed the classified archives seeking redemption in alternate choices not taken, simulations affirming resurrecting the lost multiverse might birth peace instead of war.

Endless hours Aluta spent running iterative models of reality, tweaking infinite variables of societies and souls, desperate for timelines where rebirth did not spawn catastrophe.

Aluta sought refuge in the ocean's embrace during the midnight silence, beneath a starry sky that appeared to contain the mysteries of the cosmos. The soothing effects of the water soothed his restless soul. The motion of swimming was more to him than a mere physical activity; it was a form of meditation, a quest for understanding among profound ambiguity.

Reflecting Aluta's inner anguish was the enormous and enigmatic ocean. Stroking the pen more and farther into his mind, he struggled to make sense of the enormous choice that was before him. He could not resist the allure of bringing the multiverse back to life, with all its many inhabitants and their civilizations.

He drifted, staring up at the heavenly vault, when suddenly Zara, Q, and X were at his side, a reassuring reminder of the connections that had endured through the ages. They were always there for him in his time of need simultaneously friends and mentors.

The wise and majestic Zara spoke first, her voice harmonising with the ocean's beat. "Aluta, the path you contemplate is fraught with peril. The resurrection of the multiverse is not just a rebirth of diversity but a potential resurgence of past conflicts. You must weigh the promise of what could be against the shadows of what was."

Q commented, "The fabric of reality is delicate, Aluta. Every action, especially one as significant as this, creates ripples that extend far beyond our understanding. The multiverse you long for may not be the one you revive."

X provided different perspectives. "In the infinite dance of the cosmos, each step is a choice. To resurrect is to take responsibility for all that follows. The past is a tapestry of lessons, Aluta. Are we to weave it anew, or learn from its patterns and create a different future?"

The words they spoke weighed heavily on Aluta's heart as he listened. Beyond their role as protectors of the Orca Roads, they also served as custodians of age-old knowledge. Aluta gained the insight he needed from their advice.

Aluta came to the realisation as the discourse faded that his choice would affect the fate of innumerable people, not only himself. A cosmic crossroads existed at the decision between reviving a dormant past and sustaining a present that had discovered tranquilly in conformity.

Aluta took a long breath and made his decision. As his friends looked on, the water became a witness to his determination. Aluta, Guardian of the Orca Roads, welcomed the route that lay ahead in the stillness of the night, as the cosmos held its breath. The path was defined by wisdom, courage, and the endless quest for balance in the ever-shifting dance of reality.

Sitting on the shores of reflection, Aluta felt his decision inscribed deep inside his heart as the dawn's first light bathed the sky in shades of pink and gold. Not only had the advice of the night shown him the way, but it had also encouraged him to reflect on the weight of duty that was now upon him. He had a responsibility to the future of the universe beyond that of a mere protector of the Orca Roads.

As Aluta approached the Museum of War's Guardian, Jabari stood at the door, ready to greet him. Artefacts and stories from long-vanished civilizations were on display at the museum, a sombre reminder of the horrors of the multiverse war. Along the halls, they passed exhibits that told the stories of extinct creatures and civilizations that had once flourished in the cosmic tapestry but were now just echoes in the record books.

His knowledge was based on the lessons learned in the conflict, and Jabari's presence brought the past and the present together. "Aluta I know why you're here," he said, his voice quiet but powerful, "code 17 backup of the multiverse is sacred. It is not just data; it is the legacy of countless lives, dreams, and aspirations. To resurrect it is to invite the spectre of the past into the present."

The seriousness in Jabari's eyes showed in his nod as he agreed. "But is not there value in diversity, Jabari? In the multitude of perspectives and experiences that these civilizations brought? The war was a tragedy, but it was born of ambition and fear, not the diversity itself."

Sybil, the museum's chief curator, met Aluta and Jabari at the entrance to the main archives, her normally upbeat demeanour now marked by a nervous sense of urgency. "The surveillance orb detected you accessing the Vortex Engineers records without clearance," she sternly stated. "You know those classified databases are restricted without executive sanction."

Uncomfortably, Jabari moved in response to his peer's intense stare. "Sybil, I can explain—" he started, but Sybil interrupted him. "Stop being so condescending. You are misusing your role as Records Guardian by dealing with this - this outsider," Sybil pointed accusingly at Aluta. "Who knows what sensitive data he now possesses?"

Aluta extended a hand in a gesture of peace. "Chief Curator, my interest was solely in studying extinct cultures to search for pathways to prevent future tragedies—" Sybil said with disdain. "Lofty words after getting caught red-handed violating security protocols. Or did you expect special treatment?"

The tone pissed off Jabari. "His intentions were scholarly, nothing more malicious than that. In any era of stagnation, revisiting forbidden knowledge can be instrumental to progress."

Sybil's fury grew as she approached them her eyes widened. "You betray your role as Guardian of this museum and everything it stands for by suggesting our society is somehow stagnant," she said with a sinister tone as she turned on her heel, her leaving remarks lingering in the air. "Expect a full inquiry on your misconduct from the executive commission shortly."

Jabari, who felt both indignant and deflated, watched as she left. Aluta was there to put a reassuring hand on his shoulder. With a heavy sigh, Jabari expressed his unavoidable internal struggle between his responsibilities and his aspirations, which would only intensify going forward. "She serves the past while you serve the future, my friend. This was inevitable."

With centuries pressing down on him, Jabari let out a heavy sigh. "True, diversity is the universe's strength. But it is also its greatest challenge. The balance is delicate, Aluta. What you propose could either be a renaissance of cosmic proportions or a repeat of history's darkest hour."

As they rambled on about the halls of history, Aluta took in every word, every silent witness to the successes and mistakes of yesteryear. Rather than being a simple repository for artefacts, the museum served as a furnace for the accumulation of knowledge and insight.

Aluta arrived at the core of the museum where the multiverse's code was protected. A still, powerful energy coursed through the room, and the atmosphere was heavy with the promise of what might be possible. Within this sacred space, the potential of the multiverse lay dormant, patiently anticipating the event that would set it free.

As their eyes locked, a subtle understanding flowed between Jabari and Aluta. "Whatever you decide, Aluta, know that it will shape not just your destiny, but that of all existence. The road you choose must be walked with the utmost care and reverence for the dynamic balance of all things."

Aluta and Jabari were enjoying some quiet time together in the lawn next to the Museum as the sun set, casting a rainbow of oranges and purples across the sky. In sharp contrast to the museum's sombre exhibits, the air was light with the aroma of exotic flowers.

Philosophies, historical figures, and the complex wonders of the universe were just a few of the subjects that swept them along as the evening progressed. Thanks to his extensive and profound knowledge,

Jabari's stories provided glimpses into other realms. The Guardian's magnetic personality and sharp mind made Aluta feel like they belonged together.

They started to develop a bond that went beyond words as the stars started to shine in the sky. They were able to escape the stresses of life by being in each other's company. Their talk shifted into soothing silences as the evening air, now cooler, seemed to draw them closer.

A powerful and unexpected attraction developed between them as their link grew stronger in the stillness of the night. Their embrace was an intimate union of spirit, a fiery expression of love and vulnerability.

Aluta and Jabari sat together in the inner sanctum of the museum after their shared night, as the first light of dawn shed a gentle glow over the horizon. As if it were aware of the crucial occasion taking place within its walls, the space resounded with the weight of antiquities and recollections of long-vanished civilizations.

Jabari was hesitant to approach the locked vault that held the code, even though his faith in Aluta had grown stronger due to their bond. He bore the brunt of the past and all of the associated responsibilities. In an attempt to find comfort, he looked over to Aluta. "Aluta, code 17... is more than just data. It is the echo of a thousand worlds, each with its own tales, triumphs, and tragedies. Are you certain this is the path we should tread?"

Aluta looked into Jabari's eyes with an intensity that betrayed his inner anguish, his resolve fortified by the night's reflections. "Jabari, I understand the gravity of what we are about to do. But the multiverse was more than just diverse civilizations; it was a symphony of life, of possibilities. In its absence, we have lost something integral. We have lost the vibrancy that challenges, that inspires. I believe in a future where we can learn from the past, not just hide from it."

After what seemed like an endless pause, Jabari entered the security numbers with a shaky palm and a slow nod. Code 17's storage space became visible when the vault's door swung open in response to a succession of mechanical clicks.

With a warning, Jabari clutched his arm. "I decrypted additional records on the Type VII Civ that detail why they constructed this sealed archive in first place - the cultures we are about to restore nearly shattered reality through misuse of infinite energy sources and weaponized black holes."

Despite turning pale in response to the news, Aluta clenched his jaw in resolve. "Yes, they sound very sophisticated. However, is complete forgetfulness preferable to the risk of harm?" Jabari asked with a hint of urgency. "You must understand the scale of threat here! Our universe could have been one of the casualties had the Type VII Civ not interceded!"

He called forth a string of unsettling holo-records, including stars vanishing into thin air, wormholes spewing violent singularities, and cyborg killers brandishing fractal blades as they emerged from tesseract gates. "These beings were masters of weaponizing infinity itself! If even a fraction of that power is inherited..."

The terrifying views made Aluta furrow her brow. Recapturing such omniversal power posed serious risks for revived civilizations. However, he did not waver in his beliefs. "The risks are outweighed by the wonder they could create or rediscover. We cannot let past sins condemn unborn generations who might rebuild brighter futures instead..."

The chasm between Jabari's realism and Aluta's romanticism was never wider than when the guardian lovers met eyes. The outcome of this crucial discussion over the purity versus security of existence will determine the fate of unseen cosmic seeds all around them. In that tense room, an unseen myriad of possibilities waited anxiously, their destiny hanging precariously in the balance.

With a mix of excitement and terror in his heart, Aluta took a step forward. The code, which consisted of a web of intricate algorithms and data streams, made him realise that the future was full of unknowns. However, a hope for a revived multiverse remained dormant inside him; there, the fabric of reality might be rewoven with more colour and life than before.

Aluta and Jabari stood together in the control room of the Vortex Engineers' most advanced computational nexus as they neared the culmination of their daring undertaking. Nervous excitement pervaded the room as the machine readied itself to carry out a command that would go down in multiverse history as the only sound was a low hum.

With a quiver in her hand, Aluta leaned over the genetic interface of the vault. At this pinnacle of perfection, the multiverse he had lamented would spring to life once more, giving rise to miraculous offspring. The air was electric with the weight of fate and peril, with opportunities shining brightly alongside the shadow of certain doom.

Jabari clenched his fist, his face contorted. "Once that sequence initiates, we will forever cross the event horizon, my love," he said, delicately. Looking into his eyes, Aluta could see the crucial moment when their solitary spirits had united and formed an unbreakable cosmic tie. "Are you truly ready for such creation?" he asked.

Aluta smashed his palm against the pad, his sudden decisiveness shaped by that memory. As reality started to adjust to his desires, machinery made a foreboding purr. Holograms sprang into view, showing virtual Big Bangs poised to burst into existence, embryonic galaxies seeded with elemental chemicals and chance.

Breathing in a sense of accomplishment, Aluta watched as endless possibilities swirled in the virtual world. "We are parents now, of an entire multiverse renewed," Jabari said with a ferocious embrace. In this hidden dimension, they found constellations of living civilizations preserved forever in unseen heavens, like fiery jewels of suns kindled in an invisible firmament, which future generations would one day find and marvel at. Recounting tales that were more magnificent than anything each guardian could have envisioned had reoiled fate's loom.

Jabari stood in wonder, his emotions conflicted between respect and duty. "Aluta, what have we done?... it is beyond imagination. We have given birth to a universe of possibilities, a chance for life to flourish anew."

As Aluta stared at the screen, a mix of excitement and fear washed over him. "Jabari, in this universe, I have simulated countless outcomes. Each time, diversity and peace emerged as the guiding principles. It is a testament to the strength inherent in variety, in the myriad ways life can manifest and coexist."

As he faced Jabari, Aluta made a request that would change the fabric of reality they had just created. As Aluta made his last appeal, the room, which was still buzzing with the creative energy, provided an appropriate setting.

"Jabari, my love, we have ignited the spark of a new beginning. But now, I ask you for one last act of love, a safeguard for this nascent universe. Can we hide it in the subdimensions, shield it from prying eyes and unforeseen threats, where the Vortex won't think to look?"

With a solemn nod, Jabari conveyed the seriousness of the request and the intensity of his love. "Aluta, to hide an entire universe is no small feat, but for you, for us, I will make it possible. Our universe will be a hidden gem, a secret sanctuary for life to flourish."

Aluta looked into Jabari's eyes with an intensity of thankfulness that words fail to describe. "And one more thing, Jabari. Share with this universe the mastery of time travel, bestow upon them the gift of time exploration and understanding, the ability to traverse the Orca Roads as I have."

With a balletic grace, Jabari's fingers danced over the controls. "It is done, Aluta. Our universe now rests in the folds of subdimensions, and the gift of temporal mastery is theirs. They will grow, explore, and maybe one day, they will discover us, too."

Aluta embraced Jabari in a way that was beyond space and time as he got ready to go. "In every moment of this universe's existence, I will feel your love, Jabari. You have given them—and me—a future filled with hope."

Returning to the Orca Roads, Aluta's heart a whirlwind of emotions, he planted a final, lingering kiss. Living proof of their love and an inspiration for diversity and discovery, the secret cosmos throbbed behind him.

Chapter 19
Birth of the Awakening

Aluta finds himself in the centre of the Type 19 Civilization in a place where reality itself is subject to the whims of its residents. This multiverse is a breath-taking example of the culmination of cosmic evolution; it is alive and full of all kinds of life. Here, beings who are nothing more than consciousness and idea run a cosmos that is in a perpetual state of flux.

An all-pervasive, all-knowing awareness envelops Aluta the moment he enters this limitless realm. A collective mind that amplifies the experiences, knowledge, and emotions of every being within it has superseded the concept of individuality in this civilization. The boundary between creator and created is porous in this culture; its members are godlike beings who can summon and manipulate realities with the wave of a mind. Their comprehension of the cosmos is so deep that they blend in with the consciousness that encompasses all of reality.

For these entities, the concepts of physics, time, and space are only toys. They are free from the shackles of time that bind lower societies, and they live in an everlasting peace. All of time the past, the present, and the future come together to form a single, infinite moment that includes everything that could happen or could ever happen.

Living as a society of unadulterated awareness and cognition is the way of life here. As evidence of their control over energy and information, their presence reverberates through multiple realities. By effortlessly navigating and comprehending the laws of 19-dimensional physics, they are able to harness power on an unprecedented scale. They are more than just buildings; they are expressions of ideas and intentions, intricately woven into the fabric of the multiverse, and their sheer number and size make it impossible to fathom.

Aluta has a revelation that shakes his thinking to its core as he unites with this collective mind. His identity transcends his physical body and becomes a composite of innumerable other people's ideas and experiences. In his hands are the thrilling rush of invention, the limitless delight of discovery, and the crushing weight of duty that comes with the ability to mould reality. This event makes him question his beliefs about responsibility, life, and his place in the universe, and it makes him wonder what his journey is all about and what the future holds.

In the endless consciousness, Aluta meets the Architects. As keepers of the collective consciousness, these entities exemplify knowledge that goes beyond the ages. They guide Aluta through their intricate maze, illuminating the intricate workings of the technology that unites their society in a harmonious expression of collective awareness.

A creature whose shape changes like a newborn star starts to explain the intricate workings of the system, and that being is the principal architect. "Our civilization thrives on a network of consciousness, a tapestry woven from the minds of every being within our realm," they say "The technology behind this is a marvel of quantum engineering, a system that transcends physical boundaries to link minds across the expanse of the universe."

They take Aluta through expansive halls where light streams, standing for the movement of ideas and feelings, merge into a brilliant centre. "This core," said the architect, "is the nexus of our collective consciousness. It harnesses the power of quantum entanglement, allowing for instantaneous sharing of thoughts, memories, and experiences across unimaginable distances."

The magnitude and intricacy of this achievement amaze Aluta. "But how," he questions, "do you balance the collective's needs with the individual's rights and preferences?"

An architect's figure glistens with a contemplative shade. "The framework for this balance is an inheritance from our predecessors, the gods of the Universe the Vortex. They laid the groundwork for a system that respects both the collective and the individual."

"In our society," says a different architect, "individual preferences and rights are not subsumed by the collective. Instead, they are amplified, respected, and integrated. Our technology allows for personal spaces within the collective mind, where individuality flourishes. We have algorithms that delicately balance personal desires with the needs of the collective, ensuring harmony without suppressing uniqueness."

This interaction between the many and the one, Aluta thinks, is precarious. "So, in essence, you have created a society where the individual and the collective coexist in harmony, each enhancing the other."

A pleasant warmth emanates from the architects as they nod in harmony. "Indeed," they confirm. "Our civilization thrives on this symbiosis. It is a dance of individuality and unity, a testament to what can be achieved when beings strive for a higher understanding of existence."

"Freedom is a tapestry of choices, is it not?" he mused aloud. "Yet I sense no chaotic beauty here - only cold uniformity." The lead Architect clicked in amusement. "You misunderstand, Traveller. Our citizens enjoy liberty without anarchy, woven into the fabric of our flawless design."

Aluta frowned, puzzled by the contradictory logic. "But how can one have liberty without the freedom to dissent or forge one's own path? Yours seems a gilded cage, an illusory freedom at best." The Architects bristled, red rays reflecting their distress. "ILLUSORY? The Collective governs through enlightened structure, not compelled by primal emotions. Only those lost in chaos see order as oppressive."

Aluta stood firm, unwilling to back down. "The most brilliant souls in my worlds were often outcasts and wanderers, their genius flowering through rebellion, not conformity. What radical minds rise here to push boundaries?" The Chief Architect's aura flared dangerously. "We have evolved beyond the fallacies you describe. Harmonized unity nurtures innovation aligned to constructive goals. Those who cannot align... must be realigned."

As he stands, Aluta's thoughts race with ideas that threaten this society's fundamental foundations. The Architects take notice of this because of his link to the limitless awareness. Unbridled and powerful, his ideas flood the public consciousness, shattering the rules that have long controlled this domain.

Upon detecting the disturbance, the Architects react with lightning speed and pinpoint accuracy. Surrounded and suddenly limited in movement, Aluta finds himself in a precarious situation. The accusation that he has violated their society's fundamental principles highlights the profound effect his ideas have had on them. The Architects feel compelled to eliminate his thoughts in order to protect the integrity of the collective consciousness.

Speaking with a blend of rebellion and hopelessness, Aluta expresses himself. "Is this the price of free thought in your civilization? To be silenced and re-aligned for challenging your constructs?"

With a serious expression on their face, one of the architects approaches him. "Aluta, your thoughts have endangered the harmony we have strived to achieve. In our society, the collective good supersedes individual dissent. Your mind must be realigned to preserve the peace we have cultivated."

The execution of Aluta's sentence—the wiping from public memory and realignment of his consciousness—will take place in a specific chamber. Standing before the assemblage, his heart burdened by the knowledge of what is to come, he sees the actual price of a culture that values conformity above individuality. The treatment, which aims to transform him into a conforming being by removing his individuality, serves as a sobering reminder of the delicate balance between a utopian and dystopian future.

Aluta remained resolute as the Architects began the erase sequence, the energy streams gradually increasing in intensity until they would finally break his mind. In his peripheral vision, the onlookers stood idly by, their minds hardwired to comply with the gestalt mind's incessant cycles of thought.

Speaking with confidence, Aluta said, "You silence me because you are afraid of change," and his words echoed through the mental framework. "But conformity has made you stale, trapped by stagnation masquerading as order! Your minds have lost the capacity for innovation."

Responding robotically, his computerised ideas harmonised with the gestalt, the Chief Architect showed no emotion. "Dissension breeds chaos. Your discordant impressions threaten systemic harmony. You will be reformatted."

The Architects were more like gardeners than builders; they cared for the collective society's psychic infrastructure. Consensus emerged when they nurtured the gestalt matrix, which contained their ideas and perceptions. With the pride of a caretaker, Inatinum, the Chief Architect of the Gestalt Nexus, nurtured the glimmering web of interconnected ideas. With perfect harmony permeating every part of the brain, any discordant signals were able to pass via the many logic circuits and eventually reach the community core.

Splicing together seemingly conflicting viewpoints until a hybrid equilibrium formed that could reverberate across the mental architecture was a careful process of nurturing. With nanometre accuracy, Inatinum's algorithms were continually looking for disturbances and filtering out unwanted signals. Isolation behind firewalls was necessary for unhappy memories or antisocial notions until their waveforms matched the dominant rhythms of the whole.

Inatinum immediately saw the danger posed by the outsider Aluta's breakdown of containment as an externally chaotic, highly diverse awareness. To maintain order, the Chief Architect had to do what was rational and start the realignment process. Recursive conditioning eliminated the noncompliant brain patterns, and Inatinum reassured the traveller gently that it was for unity.

"To construct observatories of sublime thought requires control," Inatinum explained when Aluta asked about stifling diversity. Achieving near-divine intelligence, with fractal patterns resonating through limitless mind-space, was the aim. "Undisciplined cognitions spawn turbulence. We have evolved beyond such animalistic drives." By design, only harmonious minds could occupy such magnificent futuristic churches.

"Our goal is an evolved equilibrium," he told the newcomers, «Where every thought resonates harmoniously with peers. Ugliness of destructive individualism is erased." Not everyone was amenable to such intrusive mental uniformity, but the reconciliation protocols were effective in reshaping problematic aesthetics.

Inatinum harshly tracked impressions of outliers. There had been an unanticipated threat of hive-mind contamination from the recent Traveller from primitive dimensions who was now next to Aluta, but the source had been located and was about to be removed. It would not be long until recursive conditioning moulded his recollections into mimicry. "There will be harmony as a result," Inatinum said. They were determined to protect the harmony they had worked so hard to achieve against any additional discord.

In unison, the assembly nodded their heads in agreement. It became clear to Aluta that he would have to challenge the gestalt root codes that supported this mechanical orthodoxy if he were to succeed in appealing to their repressed uniqueness. Aluta dove headfirst into the gestalt, his spirit harmonising with Zara's old melodies, resolute in his mission to reignite a flame of defiance and creativity in this sanitised world.

With unwavering determination, Aluta gazes out at them. "Even in the face of erasure," he points out, "the spirit of inquiry, exploration, adventure and the quest for truth, cannot be quelled."

Once a room full of solemn expectation, the Architects' start of the procedure fills it with the resonant ideas of Aluta. His voice resonates with everyone because of the sacrifice he made and the bravery he displayed in standing by his beliefs. He recounts his adventures, the dangers he has faced, and his steadfast dedication to equality and diversity.

"In every corner of the multiverse, in every timeline I have traversed, the richness of existence has always sprung from diversity not only in form but also cognitively," Aluta says, his voice resonating in the brains of the assembled assemblage. "The worlds you inhabit, the lives you lead, they exist because I dared to dream beyond the singularity of thought, beyond the confinement of a monolithic existence."

Among the myriad sentients and emerging entities in the room, his remarks stir a realisation similar to the waves in a cosmic pond. Everything about them—the myriad shapes and ideas they embody—is a direct outcome of what Aluta and Jabari did. In defiance of the Architect's desires for sterile uniformity, he had woven the multiverse into a dynamic tapestry of life.

A clamorous commotion starts to build, with a wide range of voices coming together for a common goal. All of the assembled entities, special in their own way, look over at the Architects. There is a palpable sense of renewed purpose in the air, a revolution is upon them.

In a shocking turn of events, the very beings and entities the Architects tried to control or as they called it cultivate to adhere to their will now hold them captive. Thanks to Aluta's sacrifice, the crowd is able to stand united in their pursuit of diversity and freedom.

In a beautiful turn of events, the architects end up being erased just as they were planning to erase Aluta. Their identities and memories fade into thin air as the procedure begins, and the crowd erupts in jubilation.

There is an undeniable air of revitalization and change in the air following the abrupt turn of events. The living and evolving things genuflect before Aluta as a sign of profound respect. Proclaiming him as their creator and God, their voices soar in harmony, a tapestry of innumerable tones and voices.

In the middle of all this love, Aluta stands and gently raises his hands in a calming gesture. "I am not your God," he proclaims with a grave sense of modesty in his voice. "I am Aluta, the Guardian. My journey has always been to safeguard diversity, to champion the freedom of existence in all its forms. I am but a steward of the cosmic balance, not a deity to be worshipped."

His denial of the heavenly title strikes a chord with the congregation. It is a lightbulb moment when it hits you: real leadership is not about controlling other people; it is about giving them the tools they need to succeed. Aluta's modesty and wisdom serve as guiding light, strengthening the group's will to create a new way.

Insight from Aluta and the knowledge of the people in the multiverse bring them together as they set out on a quest to build a new society. Unlike previous frameworks, this one is based on decentralisation principles, which guarantee that no one entity has control over others.

This group's combined efforts gave rise to a new proclamation: the Universal Declaration of Rights for Every Sentient and Emergent Being. This proclamation, a charter that upholds the rights and freedoms of all beings inside the universe, is a testimony to their common experiences. It is a declaration that diversity is beautiful, that everyone should be able to express themselves freely, and that everyone should be able to live without fear of persecution or erasure.

An air of solemn joy pervaded the enormous assembly hall, where seemingly endless space seemed to come together. A gathering of peculiar beings from every part of the multiverse gathered to observe a watershed event—the declaration of the Universal Declaration of Rights for All Sentient and Emergent Entities.

An intelligent being that radiated brightness and shimmered with a thousand suns' worth of colours was the first to advance. The voice of the entity is a symphony of "Rights of Non-Traditional Sentient Entities: We recognise and protect the rights of entities that may exist in non-traditional forms, such as distributed intelligences, multidimensional beings, or emergent consciousnesses in complex systems."

An amiable behemoth, whose form was an ecosystem in and of itself, spoke with a deep and resonant voice that proclaimed, "Rights to Energy Utilisation: We establish guidelines for the ethical and equitable use of energy, ensuring it does not lead to imbalances or exploitation within or outside our civilization."

Next, a multi-dimensional being whose very being is a web of interconnected cosmic strings said, "Planetary and Cosmic Stewardship: We embrace our responsibilities and rights associated with complete control over planetary resources, extending to cosmic stewardship to prevent resource exploitation on a universal scale."

A unified consciousness, sounding like a chorus of separate but equal voices, declared, "Multidimensional Rights and Ethics: We acknowledge entities existing in different dimensional realms, ensuring rights and ethical treatment across all dimensions of existence."

A living hologram, a tapestry of knowledge, asserted, "Information Sovereignty and Knowledge: We balance the rights to access and contribute to an infinite pool of information while maintaining individual and collective sovereignty over intellectual and cultural properties."

"Ethics of Infinite Mass Constructions: We set forth guidelines for constructing infinite mass structures, considering their impact on the universe's fabric, other civilizations, and cosmic ecosystems." The towering structure, a tribute to the mastery of mass, declared its announcement.

As the reading progressed, each entity added its own distinct voice to the proclamation. Cosmic environmental ethics, the rights and responsibilities of cosmic influence, the protection of diversity, interdimensional and temporal justice, guidelines for ethical existential alterations, universal access to enhancement technologies, and the ethics of immortality and existential continuity were among the topics discussed.

The hall was filled with an overwhelming feeling of purpose and unity as the last words were pronounced. In addition to serving as a set of rules, the proclamation was a symbol of the multiverse's inhabitants' determination to build a world that valued diversity, respected all forms of life, and upheld the rights of all creatures.

Chapter 20
The Cosmic Veil Lifted

Those who had played a significant role in Aluta's voyage, such Selassie, Amara, Jabari, and others, reappeared as if drawn to meet him as he neared the glistening fortress of the Type XX beings. The vast expanse of cosmic time had altered their titles and the profundity of their understanding, but their demeanour remained unaltered.

"Did you think the millenniums would make us forget our dearest friend?" In a warm embrace, Selassie hugged Aluta and giggled. "We knew this summit approached and made arrangements to meet you here." Amara gave a subtle nod, her wrist throbbing with a complex chrono-artifact. "The secrets of the Watcher's Sanctum are hidden to most, but not to your devoted allies."

They marched side by side, following their former buddy, to the lofty spires that were reserved for the highest council. In the course of his travels, Aluta became aware of the remarkable accomplishments of his companions. For example, Selassie had transformed energy designs for developing universal clusters, Amara had been an early proponent of quantum consciousness models, and Jabari had designed everlasting archives to house obscure histories.

He embraced Ayomi, the First Scholar of the Type II Civilization, whose discoveries about how to use stellar energies had helped their world achieve greater equilibrium. She now led an ark-ship that journeyed to stars that were about to collapse so that she might gather their elemental wrath and turn it into soothing fuel. "You are the reason we became dreamers," she replied with a sincere tone.

Gliding from the Type V Fortress's silver-domed halls, Third Ethicist Wen continued to advocate for the Ministry of Planetary

Engineers' cosmic stewardship. "Two hundred bailiwicks have aligned their asteroid harvesting protocols with sustainability measures you helped draft," Wen told him with pride.

As he came up, Amina, Lerato, Ayodele, Liraz, Chidike, Makena, Dr. Zulu and Carlota each added their own colourful story to the tapestry of thanksgiving for this guardianship. Aluta responded by expressing his gratitude to them for illuminating his journey across numerous uncharted realms. The relationships they shared had moulded fate.

The visible proof of the Type XX feats, such as inverted megastructures that harness the mass-energy of entire superclusters, cosmic genome sequencing diagrams with divinity particles, xenofungal reactors that process dark photons to overcome metaphysical barriers, far outweighed those astounding successes. Aluta gasped for air as she contemplated the need for such technical and philosophical expertise.

Finally, they made it into the Chronos Sanctum, the sacred space where the keepers of Reality stood. Pride and affection were visible on Selassie's face as he held Aluta's shoulder. "My friend, we plotted your route at every turn. Having even a small role to play was a privilege. Act immediately - fate is beckoning. Jabari gently kissed Aluta on the lips before discreetly withdrawing. "We will welcome you home with celebrations when you return - as the man who met existence itself and came back with its truths."

Aluta was able to transcend the last boundary and meet his apotheosis because his friends were believing in him. Shapes he could never have imagined blossomed all around him, and ideas whispered of adventures he could never have imagined. Still, X, the cosmic Watcher, was waiting at the chamber's centre, an old mystery solved. As Aluta eagerly anticipated their conversation, his pace accelerated and his trepidation dissipated. The instructor patiently awaited the student's return with bated breath.

X said, "Bonjour, Aluta," as their voices danced through space and time like a tune. Through the threads of inquisitiveness and bravery, your trip has been a carpet of revelations. After travelling the Orca Roads and seeing the rise and fall of civilizations, you must now go beyond your concerns and accept the universe as a whole.

As X looked into Aluta's eyes, they could see the light from faraway galaxies. This one moment of connection was the pinnacle of his trip, which had been filled with ups and downs, discoveries and losses. "I have been trying to figure this out, X. I have strove to understand the cosmos, safeguard it, and discover my role within it".

A gesture that extended throughout the universe, X nodded. "Aluta, you have seen things from a human perspective. On the other hand, in Type 20 space, observing turns into being, while being determines what is observed".

Quantum fluctuations that violated the laws of physics caused the air to shimmer as Q appeared. "Observation itself changes the observed in the quantum world. The cosmos is a picture of possibilities, created by the eye of the observer."

Aluta deeply listened, his emotions and ideas swirling around in a chaotic web. He thought about the paradox of observation, how the observer and observed are inseparable, and how his personal journey had moulded not only his perceptions but also the reality he had experienced.

Touched by Infinity now able to grasp all of reality, the Guardian's odyssey is not over, it just began. The Orca roads call and Aluta dives into deeper wonderous depths.

FIN

A Note About the Author

Cape Town, South Africa's Trev Dube stands out in his debut solar punk and afrofuturistic sci-fi novel. As an autodidact, polymath and interdisciplinary thinker, Trev infuses his diverse knowledge from science, art, technology, and philosophy into his narrative, creating a rich, multi-layered thought provoking and fascinating story.

His novel is a vivid portrayal of a future where technology harmoniously coexists with nature, emphasizing human and other intellectual entities' well-being and flourishing. Trev's narrative is more than a story; it's an intellectual exploration, challenging readers to engage with alternative ideologies and perspectives of possible futures and future civilisations. This interdisciplinary approach enriches his storytelling, making this novel not just a journey through a futuristic world but also an exploration of human understanding.